The Black Llama Caper

Robert Muccigrosso

Copyright © 2008 by Robert Muccigrosso

ISBN 0-7414-4739-8

Published by:

INFINITY
PUBLISHING.COM

1094 New DeHaven Street, Suite 100
West Conshohocken, PA 19428-2713
Info@buybooksontheweb.com
www.buybooksontheweb.com
Toll-free (877) BUY BOOK
Local Phone (610) 941-9999
Fax (610) 941-9959

Printed in the United States of America

Printed on Recycled Paper

Published May 2008

For Maxine

Acknowledgments

My thanks go to several people who have helped me in ways both large and small. Bob Cawley, a gifted mentor, has given me many useful suggestions and warm encouragement. Jane Hagus and Joyce Brennan have also aided me in my work. A special thank-you goes to my good friend Mitch Phillips, who read my manuscript and spent numerous hours helping me to wrestle with thorny computer problems. Last but certainly not least, my gratitude once again goes to my wonderful wife Maxine for her forbearance, but most of all for her love.

1

Business was slower than my ex-wife's moron brother. I told my secretary Dotty to take the rest of the afternoon off and get her nails done. Watching her gnaw on her cuticles made me both hungry and fearful that she'd start on mine if she didn't get out of the place. I kept hoping that a new client would show, but why would he? There hadn't been one since I bought myself a decent tie. So I locked my Smith & Wesson .38 special in the file cabinet, put on my coat and fedora, and left.

It was dark that night, darker than the guys who hung out on the wrong side of the tracks. Only there weren't tracks. Not in this town, at least. Come to think of it, there weren't many dark guys, either. And it was raining, raining so hard that I had to wipe my eyelashes every few minutes to see where I was going, which was to Ma's Diner for a bit of grub to help me forget another forgettable day.

Ma's was almost deserted when I got there. It wasn't the hour. It was the food. The grub wasn't actually so bad as long as you stuck to basics like sandwiches with nothing between the slices and vegetables that you brought cooked from home. But it was cheap, and without a case in more than a month, cheap was good enough for me.

I took a seat at the counter and whistled for Betty the waitress. Betty took her sweet time sashaying over to me. For some reason she was still sore, convinced that I had stolen her tip a few weeks ago. Some nerve! Sure, I had stiffed her on more than one occasion, but palm her tip? I hadn't stooped that low. At least not yet.

"Yeah? Whatta you want, Mr. Big Shot Gumshoe?"

"I know what I don't want, honey, and that's more of your over-painted lip. Now be nice to me or I'll tell Ma that it was you who licked the meringue off the lemon pie a few days ago."

She got flustered. "All right, all right. I'll make nice with you. Now whatta you want?"

I rummaged for change in my trousers, found a lot of lint, and decided that a porterhouse wasn't in the cards. "I'll have a slab of apple pie and a cuppa java. Oh, and a piece of cheese."

"You want the cheese on the pie or in a trap?"

I felt like slapping her zits-pocked face but remembered that my mother had told me always to be a gentleman, along with all sorts of other useless advice that didn't get you farther than the nearest fire hydrant. So I just glared at her and told her to make it snappy because I was working on a big one. I lied. So what? In my profession lying is as important as cleanliness and godliness are to soft-hearted suckers.

While I was pondering life's mysteries and waiting for my chow and coffee, a husky voice asked, "Is this stool taken, handsome?" Swiveling around, I expected to find that the voice belonged either to Mike Stepanowski, known to his closest friends as "Stepanowski," or Bernard "Bernie the Brioche" Eppinger. But I knew that Stepanowski was dead and that I had never met Eppinger.

"If you don't want company," the voice said, "I'll wait for another empty counter seat." I should have known then that trouble lay ahead, since all the other counter seats were empty. In fact, the whole place was empty, save for Betty and some short order cook in the back whose hands were as dirty as Al Capone's. Should have, could have. Too late.

"Sure, babe," I said, "pull up a stool and take some weight off your bunions." (I had developed a real way with words after my home correspondence course with Vinny the Vocabulary Man.)

"Thanks," she said, "I think I will."

I could see that she also had a way with words, but that was not her chief attraction. She was a real looker, though not necessarily a good looker. Her chin receded well into her neck, her eczema had not cleared up, and her nose hairs stuck out. But still there was something, a certain je ne sais squat.

We looked at each other without speaking for a full three or four seconds. It had been a long time, maybe even a couple of years, since I'd been with a woman, but I still knew how to pitch the old blarney. "Wanna see a menu?" I crooned.

"I just need a strong shoulder to cry on, big guy. How's your shoulder tonight?"

I told her that I had been having some stiffness ever since slugging a dame who had refused to include the cost of a pastrami on rye, with pickle but light on the mustard, with the tab for my investigative services, and that my mother's uncle Gregor had had bursitis and so it might run in the family, and that . . .

Noticing that her eyes had closed and that her head was nodding, exposing the blond roots of her black hair, I asked, "Hey, lady, are you all right?"

"Sure, sure," she said soothingly. "I was just resting my eyes." Then she turned those orbs, one blue, the other brown, on me and moaned, "I'm so tired. I have to go home and rest. Would you like to accompany me and lie down for a while?"

I wasn't tired but what the hell. Maybe it was the feminine way she picked her nose. Maybe it was her exotic odor. "Yeah, I don't mind. But I gotta finish my pie first. Wanna piece?"

She snickered and seemed about to reply but gave me a knowing smile instead. We didn't exchange more than a few words in the half hour it took Betty to serve the slop and me to finish it off. "All set." I grinned. "And now for a little rest back at your place, or as the Frenchies say, 'chez twat'."

I waved good-bye to Betty and left her a coin and some lint as a tip. I was feeling generous and excited about the adventure that lay ahead.

Outside the rain had slackened to a downpour. My lady friend—I hadn't yet asked her name—suggested a taxi. "How far away do you live?"

"About a mile or two from here."

I made a rapid calculation of the taxi fare. "Oh, that's nothing. The walk will do us good. And we can walk fast since there's no one on the streets." I did feel a bit cheap and also sorry that the lady wasn't wearing a coat, but so what? Life's just one struggle after another. Besides, the walk would give me plenty of time to figure out how I wanted the evening to play out.

We got to her place, a fifth-floor walk-up whose stairs creaked like a quarterback's knees after a dozen seasons on the job. We were drenched, she especially. "I'll just put on a wrapper," she said.

"Fine," I said. "I'll just make myself at home." "Home" was sparsely furnished. An enlarged photo of a man captioned "landlord" pretty much covered one wall. I noticed that the photo had what appeared to be bullet holes in it. A small bookcase highlighted another wall. It held only three works: *Beat It*, by Dominique Dominatrix; *You Are Who You Eat*, by Lusty Lustig; and *The Sayings of Saint Theresa*. Something seemed odd, but I couldn't put my finger on it. What appeared to be a pair of men's undershorts was stuffed between the cushions of a badly stained ecru sofa, and that was odd. What had the lady been doing wearing a pair of men's shorts, especially one decorated with purple unicorns? And why were the shorts on the sofa rather than on a chair? My years as a private dick had put me on the scent of possible foul play. A dick's nose knows.

Then, before I could say—let alone spell—antidisestablishmentarianism, she appeared. "How would

4

you like it, mister?" She had changed out of her wet clothes into a kimono that she had forgotten to tie. I was about to tie it for her, but for the life of me couldn't remember whether a Matthew Walker, Clove knit, or Fisherman's bend was the best knot to use.

The fact is I didn't know for sure what she was getting at. What was it? My gray cells raced to discover the answer to her puzzling question before it was too late, especially since I had a long day ahead waiting for clients who would never show. "I'm not sure what you're getting at, sister, but it better be good. I've had a rough day. The pie and cheese were as stale as last year's news and the coffee as thick as dirt mixed with water. I got no time for games. What do you mean 'How would you like it?'"

She looked at me with her mouth open. I hadn't noticed before that she had no teeth. "Are you for real?"

I could have flipped her my private eye's license or driver's license or even my membership in the YMCA, but thought better of it. I didn't like what she asked or how she asked it or, for that matter, the color of her kimono. This dame's bananas, I told myself. She doesn't even know that I'm real. I put on my left shoe, which I had removed upon entering the apartment. It was still soppy, although probably not as much as the right one, which I had lost somewhere after we left Ma's. I would have put on my hat and coat too, until I remembered that I hadn't taken them off.

"Well," I said, "I guess this is good-bye. It's too bad. I thought for a moment that we had something really special."

I half hoped that she would try to stop me, that she would say something, that she would throw herself at my wet feet and beg me not to leave, or at least to have a nosh before I left. But life doesn't always have a happy ending. She just stood there gumming on some sugar-coated peanuts. She didn't offer me any. Not one. And they are my favorites. I nodded to her, opened the door, went down the stairs and out into the night. The rain was by now just a mean, hard drizzle. I didn't realize then that tomorrow I'd be in the path of a hurricane.

2

I awoke with the taste of fried anchovies in my mouth. Maybe it was the effects of the chow I had gulped down at Ma's last evening or maybe just the dim recollection of what had transpired at what's-her- face's. Yeah. I couldn't forget that. No dame had ever eaten sugar-coated peanuts without offering me any.

But that was yesterday and today is . . . I reached under the covers and pulled out my calendar. I keep it there because I like to sleep with dates. It was Saturday. An early November Saturday. And it was chilly. The landlord never gave me heat except when I was late paying rent, which was not more than once a month. I thought about staying in bed and keeping warm under the covers, but I knew that the early worm catches birds, and this worm needed some clients fast. I had a slight hunch, very slight, that today might be my lucky day and that a well-heeled client would show. And I knew that as long as there are shoemakers in this town, there'll always be a well-heeled client walking the streets.

I pulled off the covers and my Dr. Dentons and stumbled to the bathroom. I thought hard and long about brushing my teeth but thought better of it. Too much brushing would take the enamel off those bright lights. I showered quickly, lathered my face, and shaved off three days of stubble, along with some skin. Then I carefully chose the underwear, socks, suit, shirt and tie that I had been wearing since Tuesday. Looking into the mirror, I told myself that I could do worse.

I decided to fix breakfast today. Usually I eat on the run, but too many food and coffee stains on my clothes and endless cases of acute indigestion had told me something, although I can't recall exactly what. In any case, I made myself of pot of java and gulped most of it down along with a peanut butter and salami sandwich like the ones my mom used to give me as a special treat. I left the dirty plate for later, figuring that the roaches needed to eat too. Careful not to step in the puddles, I picked up my coat and fedora from the floor and left my small but cozy abode.

The rain had stopped and the sun had begun to wink at the city. Maybe today is the day, I thought, and Lady Luck's big blue ones might fix on me. Yeah, I even began to whistle as I walked to my office. I was halfway there when I felt something strange. Hell! I had forgotten to put on my shoes. I thought of going back for them but realized that I had lost one shoe in last night's downpour and the other was still drying in my oven. So I pressed on, remembering that I had an old pair of sneakers in my office that went with everything.

I reached my office building, said good morning to Joe the elevator man, and walked up the eight stories to my place of business. I glanced at the sign painted on my door: "Dick DeWitt, Privates Investigator." I had long ago demanded that the landord get rid of the extra letter, but the scuzzbag hadn't. Each time I saw the sign I recalled how mad Mom had been when I legally changed my name, which had seemed too long and ungainly. After all, who would want to hire a tec named "Richard DeWitt"? Come to think of it, who'd want to hire me at all, I pondered as I opened the door, switched on the light, and prepared for another day of being closer to the grave. This sort of gloominess sometimes stuck in my craw the way this morning's peanut butter and salami sandwich was doing.

The office was a mess. Dotty's fingernail bits were all over the place, and her bra was hanging from the old

Remington on which she could type a nifty ten or twelve words a minute. As typists go that ain't much, but Dotty was a good girl and plenty loyal. She had had an offer to work in her cousin Elmer's glue factory but had turned it down to stay with me. "I've been with you almost three years, Mr. DeWitt," she had said, "and another three or so won't hurt, although I do wish you'd pay me more than a few times a year." Pay her? Huh! With business the way it was during these hard times, I was lucky I could pay myself occasionally. And with that dark thought in mind I sat down behind my battered secretary—the desk, that is, not Dotty—remembering just in the nick of time that I needed a chair.

10:45. No calls, no clients. I kept reading the newspaper I had swiped from the office across the way. "President says the worst is over and that good times lie ahead." Sure, sure. "Unemployment still high." "Society matron breaks leg tripping over bum in gutter." I turned to the racing section and noticed that the horse I had been thinking of betting on came in at 30 to 1 odds. It's a dog's world, I thought, and promised myself that I'd switch to greyhounds the next time I had a shekel or two.

Suddenly I heard a tapping at the door. I knew it wasn't a raven. A raven's tap is lighter because its claws are turned slightly inward during the fall and winter seasons. Reaching into the file drawer for my trusty .38, I told whoever it was to come in.

He was slightly under average height, maybe five-four or so, and slightly above average weight, maybe 210. There was nothing unusual about his face either, save for the monocle he wore in each eye. Nor about his garb: brown slacks, blue blazer, orange tie, Philadelphia Phillies baseball cap.

I pointed to the chair that faced me across the desk and told him to sit down and take a load off his toes, all ten of them.

He seemed nervous, maybe because he couldn't remove the load from his toes or maybe because there were more than ten of them. "Sir," he squeaked, "I need help bad, and I hear that while you're not the best gumshoe in the city—far from it, they tell me—you're probably the cheapest." He looked at me pleadingly through his monocles. They were wet, either from his tears or from the water that had begun to drip from the ceiling as a result of yesterday's rain.

A natty dresser who also wears monocles must have a lot of dough, I figured. Whatever his problem, I couldn't afford to lose this Beau Brummell.

"Well you've come to the right place, Mr. . . . er . . . "

"Baker," replied the monocles.

"And what do you do, if I may ask, Mr. Baker?"

"I bake."

My instincts, as usual, were right on the money. He does have a lot of dough.

I knew I had to grill him hard if I wanted to get the case. "Can you be more specific? What exactly do you bake? Bread? Cupcakes? Sacher tortes? Blackbirds in a pie?"

"A little of this and a little of that. But it's not about my work that I've come to see you. It's about my girl Mona. I think that there's something going on."

You can always *cherchez* the femme, I thought, and also look for her.

"Mr. Baker, what exactly do you think is going on?" I eyed the poor chump and could tell that he would have difficulty giving me the low-down, unless he removed the monocle that had slipped into his mouth.

"I think Mona Tuvachevsky-Smith—that's her name—has been kidnapped and is being held for ransom," he sputtered.

I looked across the desk straight into his monocle. The one that still seemed glued to his eye. "What makes you think that she's been kidnapped, Mr. Baker? Have you received a ransom note?"

"No, but I did receive a call last evening. No one spoke. Only there was a lot of heavy breathing."

"Hold on," I told him. "That's not proof of any foul play. Maybe Ma Bell gave you a bad connection or maybe the caller was only trying to stop his hiccups." But deep down in my brain I knew Baker was right: foul play had taken place, and the damsel was in distress.

"I'll tell you what I'm gonna do. I'm really tied up with plenty of work these days, but you seem like such a nice guy, I'm going to take the case and find little Mona for you."

The poor man turned ashen. "There's something you ought to know, Mr. DimWitt. Mona's not so little. She's six-five in her stocking feet."

I didn't like that and I told him so. First of all, the little twerp had got my name wrong. And second, who's he kidding? What kind of dame that size can't take care of herself?

"I'm sorry, Mr. DeWitt, but she can't fend for herself. You see, she's so tall that she gets dizzy every time she looks down, which is pretty much all the time."

"Well, she's sort of a horse of a different color then," I said as I tried to soothe his ruffian feathers. "Any leads for me to go by? Any enemies? Maybe someone who'd like to cut her down to size? Do you think some basketball team wanted her? How about the Harlem Globetrotters? Did she have a tan? Or maybe the House of David. Did she have a beard?"

The poor bastard just shook his head. "No, she's a fair-skinned blonde. She did used to have a beard, but it kept scratching my monocles when she stooped to kiss me and so she shaved it off about a month ago without my having to ask. Oh, she was special, my poor lost Mona."

"Okay, okay. I get the picture. What about work or places she liked to frequent?"

"She used to work as a bouncer at Happy Hooligan's over on 10th and Boozer Boulevard but had to quit and lay low after some guy hit on her and she stuck a martini, glass and all, up his . . . well, you know." His brows began to furrow and I could see that the monocle was causing some blood to flow. "She did go to the museum a lot, especially after she lost her job. I know that she adored the moderns. She said that seeing their paintings made her feel ten feet tall, although why she needed to feel taller than she is I don't know."

I looked up from the pad on which I had been furiously doodling as he spoke. "I'll check this out," I promised. "Anything else you can think of?"

He scratched his head vigorously, and I ducked as the dandruff flew my way. "Well, as of late she has been going to a certain Chinese restaurant, the Jaded Pavilion over on Shadow Lane. But whenever I asked if we could go there together, she'd give some excuse, like she'd been there just a few days ago or that she heard it was closed by order of the Board of Health." He paused. "Does that sound a little suspicious to you, Mr. DeWitt?"

"Not in the least," I lied to reassure him. I hadn't had chink food in a cat's age, and that was as good a reason as any—better, in fact—to follow up on the lead. "Mr. Baker, I'm your man. Now as for my fees and expenses . . . "

He cut me off faster than my ex-wife had when I tried to explain the traces of lipstick on my trousers. "Please, sir," he began to sob, "I'm not a wealthy man, although I make a living, but—and I'll tell you this if you can keep a secret— I'm due to come into a lot of moolah as soon as they read the will that my dear departed Uncle Ebeneezer Baker left when he died a few days ago in Perth, Australia. He made his money in sheep rustling and swindling aborigines out of their seashells." He paused. "And you can be sure, Mr. DeWitt, that you'll share in my good fortune once you find little Mona."

"I know that your word is as good as the next man's, Mr. Baker, and I'm sure you'll do the right thing." We shook hands on our gentlemen's agreement and exchanged good-byes.

Had I made a mistake, I wondered, by not demanding some money right then and there or at least getting him to sign a chit? Maybe. But beggars can't be choosy, and this worm had his bird in hand. Besides, I had quietly picked up the monocle that had fallen to the floor and was holding it as collateral.

3

The wind was picking up as I headed for the Jaded Pavilion to search for Mona and to grab some lunch, although not necessarily in that order. I turned my coat collar up and made the twenty-block trip from my office to the restaurant in good time.

The chink eatery looked dilapidated from the outside and predictably proved a dump inside. The frayed, discolored leaves of an ancient potted palm slapped my face as I opened the door. I returned the favor, flooring and then kicking it repeatedly. My toes hurt, but I think the plant got the worst of it.

I was hoping for some slit-skirted broad to slink up to me with a menu in hand and show me to a table. Any table. None of them were occupied. I waited, but no broad. After a quarter hour or so I concluded that actions speak louder than words, unless, of course, you're yelling yourself hoarse. I picked up a dish that held some stale chop suey breathing its last and hurled it out the nearest window.

The doors of the kitchen swung open. "Hey, what you do that for?" an angry voice called. "That food for tonight's guests." As he drew nearer, I could see that the voice belonged to an older man, say, eighty or so, who was brandishing a hatchet in one hand and a dead furry animal in the other. I reached for my .38 but realized that I had left it in the office. Damn! I had to think fast. My Boy Scout training hadn't taught me much else than how to tie knots and play strange games with my scoutmaster. And I hadn't used my fists since I pummeled my ex-brother-in-law for taking the last pork chop one night when he was cadging a meal off his sister and me. I figured it was time to play cut or run: Confucius with a cleaver would cut if I didn't run.

"Easy, old man," I cautioned. "I was just admiring the chop suey, especially with all those little things moving around in it, and the plate just slipped out of my hand."

"Okay, Mr. Lound Eyes, for minute I think you clazee but now understand. Likee sit down?"

I breathed a sigh of relief, nodded, and followed him to the farthest table, the one next to the sign that read: "No likee food? Tough." Years of experience and instinct told me that this was not your everyday chink restaurant.

"What you like?"

"Lemme see," I said. "I'll have some wonton soup."

"No have it."

"Then I'll settle for the egg drop."

"No have it."

By this time I almost regretted that I hadn't gone to Ma's for lunch. "Well, what kind of soup do you have?"

Canton Charlie thought for a moment and played with his pigtail. He was totally bald on top but wore the pigtail wrapped around his neck. "We have Flench onion, Mulligatawny, and Campbell's tomato. Which one you like?"

"Forget it," I said. I'll just have Colonel Tso's chicken."

"Colonel Tso no wok here any more. He go home to Egypt. But we have Major Ho's hose meat. It velly good."

"Just bring me some fried rice and some tea," I said.

A half hour passed. No patrons entered the joint, but weird sounds were coming from the kitchen. I could have sworn that I heard someone dribbling a basketball and cursing in a high-pitched voice. I was suspicious but reminded myself that I had to concentrate on finding Mona.

Charlie finally shuffled back with my order. I wished that he hadn't used his fingers to mix the tea with the rice, but by this time I could have eaten anything. And probably was about to do so. I scarfed down the meal. Charlie was sitting by himself in a corner, puffing on a cigarette that didn't smell like any ordinary tobacco, if you get my drift. And I sure got his, as it wafted across the empty room.

"Hey, Charlie," I called, "I'm finished with this poison. Bring the check."

Charlie stumbled back to the kitchen and after another seeming half hour or so stumbled back with the check and a fortune cookie. "Lead the fortune, lead the fortune," he urged.

The cookie was so stale that I had to use the blackjack I always carry in my hip pocket to crack it open. "You will soon meet a black llama. Beware." Now I knew I was getting somewhere on the Mona case. I took out a fin and caressed it between my fingers to show Charlie what he could expect if he rolled dice with me. The fiver fell into what remained of the fried rice and tea. Charlie went for it, but I beat him over the hand with my blackjack before he could grab it.

"Now listen, old man, before I play my rendition of 'Chinatown, My Chinatown,' on your ugly bald head and tattoo a picture of Anna May Wong on your hairless chest, I want some information," I cooed, figuring to nice-talk him before getting tough.

He was trembling. I realized I was standing on his foot. He looked around to make certain no one else was there. "Sure, sure, I give you inflammation." He was sweating a lot. "Wha you wanna know, misser?"

"Ever seen this dame?" I asked as I reached into my pocket for a snapshot of Mona. Then I realized that I had forgotten to get one from my client.

"I never saw her," Charlie whined. I could tell that he was eager to answer my question. Maybe too eager.

"Did a real tall dame with a thing for basketball ever have the bad luck to eat in this greasy spoon?"

He said the restaurant only used greasy chopsticks, not greasy spoons.

"Don't get wise with me," I snarled and raised my blackjack.

"Only makee jokee," he cried.

"You better make nicee, Charlie, or else. Have you seen her or haven't you?"

"Maybe . . . " The chink had been about to say something when he fell to the floor. Green slime was oozing from his mouth. It was probably something he ate, I concluded, sorry that my stomach was also trying to digest what passed for food here but not necessarily elsewhere. He gasped for breath and motioned for me to come near. I took off my jacket for fear that he would spew some green stuff onto it and moved my ear close to his mouth. I could smell his stinking breath, which also tickled my ear.

"The woman . . . the woman, she . . . "

I shook him violently and then kicked him in the ribs just in case he was playing possum. But he wasn't. Those few words he had mumbled were the last that anyone was ever going to hear from him. Someone had put out the chink's lights. I stood up, reached for one of the soiled napkins—they were all soiled—and draped it over the poor bastard's face. Then I pocketed the fiver, which I had intended to do in any case, gave the potted palm another good kick, and went out the door. The wind was still blowing hard, but I had miles to go before I slept. Mona, I'm going to find you, baby, or my name isn't Dick DeWitt.

4

The afternoon was hoarding a couple of hours, enough time to follow up on the client's second lead and visit the museum. It was located across town. With the wind stiffening by the minute, I decided to hail a bus, which I managed to catch after chasing it for at least a dozen blocks. I boarded it, greeted the driver with a few choice words that caused him to clench his teeth, and dropped a nickel into the slot. Both he and the slot deserved a slug.

An elderly lady on the bus noticed that I was having trouble catching my breath and offered me her seat before I could ask for it. Grateful and always the gentleman, I was about to tip my fedora to her but noticed that I was hatless. Had I lost it chasing the bus or left it behind at the Jaded Pavilion? I continued to fret over the loss until I realized that I had missed my stop. The five-block walk back to the local temple of culture probably did me no harm. Or any good.

It had been a couple of years since I had visited the museum. Art doesn't faze me for the most part, although I do like to draw those pictures where you have to connect the dots. My mom always insisted that I had artistic talent and should have gone to Paris to study at the Sorbet. My ex, on the other hand, said that I lacked any appreciation for art and that I was a Phila Steen. (I never could figure out who this

Steen guy was and whether my wife had been shacking up with him.)

This being Saturday, admission to the museum was free, a fact that had not been lost on me when I made my decision to go there rather than back to my apartment and snooze the day away. Mona fancied modern art, according to my client. So I started with the Egyptian gallery. How the hell was I to know that the joint was showing old Egyptian exhibits rather than new ones—and revolting ones at that. I've seen a few dead ones in my day, but imagine a place of culture throwing corpses wrapped in dirty black rags into boxes that looked like coffins and calling it "art." Gimme a break!

I was tempted to call it quits, go home, and make some serious zzz's but decided to keep on the key vive, as the Frenchies said during the late war against the krauts. I stopped and questioned several people who seemed in a trance in front of various pictures. They were annoyed, maybe because I woke them or maybe they didn't like being poked in the ribs. One geezer asked me if I had no shame but backed off when I threatened to take his cane.

Finally I came across a fat guy in a uniform who appeared to perform some function. Can't fool a dick, I always say. Fatso was a guard, it turned out. I went right to the point.

"Seen any six-five blonde who might have been dribbling a basketball in front of a Picasso or Matisse," I asked?

"As a matter of fact, I did."

Bingo! "When? Is she still here?"

"It's not a she, it's a he. And get your cottonpickin' hands off my lapels or I'll call for the police."

"I am the police, fatty, so watch your mouth and your step before I trim a few inches off your waistline with my fingernail clipper."

"Sorry, sir, but with all the violent crime that goes on in a museum you can't take chances. Why just the other day some lady tried to take two museum pamphlets instead of one. She would have gotten away with them if me and another guard hadn't tackled her and broke her hip. Geez, I don't know what makes people act the way they do these days."

"All right, all right," I told him, "enough of the vicious crimes."

I reached into my pocket and he flinched. Stupid guy. I was only reaching for my business card, which I gave to him. "Here, George, take my card and give me a buzz if some big blonde dame comes in here with a basketball. There'll be something in it for you if you can square it with me." Then I handed him my museum pamphlet.

"Thanks a lot, mister. My name's not George but it is Georg. How did you know?"

I winked at him. That's something else a good gumshoe knows how to do. I also made sure not to let him see the second pamphlet, which I had swiped and hidden in my underwear. With that I said good-bye to the museum. Mona, I'll have to catch you another day, I thought. Now my tired mind and body needed to catch some shut-eye. I walked outside. The wind was still blowing briskly, but the afternoon no longer was hoarding its hours.

5

This time I caught a bus as soon as I left the museum. Unfortunately, it was the wrong one and took me out of my way. By the time I got home and crept past the landlord's ground floor apartment and up to my third-floor one, I was exhausted. There was no Fido to greet me, lick my face, and bark, "Sit down, big fellow, and make yourself at home." There was no Tabby to purr and rub against my tired legs. There were only the roaches and me. Two's company but a few hundred is more than a crowd. I had been thinking of getting a cat or a dog, or even a pet boa constrictor, but hadn't got around to it. Maybe I'd treat myself for Christmas.

Saturday night, the loneliest night of the year, lay ahead. No Sassy Sally waiting out there with outstretched arms for her gumshoe to come sweep her off her feet. No Hot Hannah putting on the last of her make-up to go out on the town with her Number One Man. So let's make the most of it, I told myself, and stop wallowing in self-pity.

I poured myself several fingers of sneaky pete, sank into my favorite easy chair—the one with the protruding springs—took off my high-top sneakers, and settled back. I put aside thoughts of Mona and turned to solving other serious puzzles, like figuring out why I played cat's cradle so poorly and why the milk that I had bought less than a month ago had gone bad. I was stumped. I took a couple of swigs of the sneaky pete. Then I took a couple more. I asked myself why I was feeling so . . .

Next thing I knew the phone was ringing. Still groggy with sleep and booze, I staggered across the room and picked up the receiver.

"Dick, is that you? Help me! Please help me!" a woman's voice begged.

"Who is this?" I asked.

"It's . . . " Then a click and the line went dead.

I was at a loss to figure out who would be calling me, asking for my help, and then hanging up. It wasn't my mom, who began every call with "How are you, sonny boy? How are they hanging?" And it sure wasn't my former wife, whose almost once-a-month calls consisted of: "Where's the alimony check, you good-for-nothing bastard?" So who was it? Could it have been Mona? That was a far-fetched thought, but I'd gone farther to fetch thoughts in other cases.

The clock read 9:17 and I wasn't in the mood to argue. Hunger was ripping at my insides. So I went to the kitchen, opened a can of Spam, and poured a lot of catsup on it—the Spam, that is, not the can. I washed it down with coffee that had been sitting around doing nothing since the morning. Then I piled all the dirty stuff in the sink, so that it could get acquainted with the week's accumulation. The sink was getting pretty full. I made a mental note to wash its contents one of these days.

Now I had a choice. I could either stay home, pour some more sneaky pete, and catch what was on the radio, or I could go to my neighborhood gin mill, have hooch poured for me, and catch hell from Gus the barman for having eaten three bowls of his free peanuts the last time I frequented the establishment. That was a no-brainer: I had no peanuts in the house. I put on my sneakers, coat, and fedora (I own several) and headed for the bar.

What I liked most about The Slippery Elbow was its lack of pretense: It didn't try to appear clean. In fact, it was filthier than my place, which was saying a lot. An inspector from the Board of Health showed up periodically but only to collect some under-the-counter bribes and a couple of beers on the house.

The clientele was great. My kind of people. Sure, a few of them were wanted for some infraction of the law or other, but nothing too serious. And what great stories they had to tell. Samuel "Southpaw Sammy" Stickit, for instance, always told how he pitched for Buffalo in the International League until a sore commissioner banned him from baseball for beaning an umpire who had objected to Sammy's slavering all over the ball. The ump probably wouldn't have beefed so much if Sammy hadn't also invited his infielders to contribute their saliva. And then there's Tony "Two-Fingers" Mangiamangia, the skinny guinea who lopped off a few of his digits while paying more attention to the meat on some broad than to the pork sausage he was preparing when he worked as a cook at Guido's Kosher Deli.

Neither Sammy nor Tony was there when I arrived. I took a stool at the bar but not before wiping the seat with Gus's bar rag. The joint was fairly crowded, although most of the regulars didn't usually show up until after 11:00 or so. Gus asked me what I wanted. I said the usual. So he brought me a bowl of peanuts. "You wanna drink too, or is this another of your freeloading nights?" I was hurt. The peanuts were stale. "Gimme a gin rickey," I told him. "Easy on the rickey, but don't stint on the gin." Gus just snorted.

While Gus was fixing my drink and mumbling something about a tab that was nearly as large as the new Empire State Building, I cased the joint. Maybe there was a good-looker looking for another good-looker, namely me. Maybe I'd get lucky tonight. It had been a while. I spotted Gardenia Gertie, who blew me a big kiss and motioned for me to join her at her table. I wasn't that desperate. Gardenia Gertie was also known as Gonorrhea Gertie to those who had gotten to know her real well. I blew a kiss back and yelled, "Not on your life!" As I said, Mom always taught me to be a gentleman.

I sipped at my gin rickey, which Gus, still mumbling, had slammed down in front of me. Some of it splashed on my shirt. Gus should be more careful, I thought.

"How ya doing, Mr. DeWitt? Long time no see."

I was ready to whip out my blackjack and beat the sonofabitch senseless for making me choke on my drink. Fortunately for him, I had left my companion back at the apartment. But as I spun around to see my assailant, I was pleasantly surprised to see the mug of none other than Light Fingers Louie, the best safecracker in town. He was a good yegg, as far as I was concerned.

"Louie, you old sonofabitch," I greeted him cordially. "How ya been? I thought you were doing five in Sing Sing."

"The years fly by, Mr. DeWitt, just like Lucky Lindy and his airplane. Actually they let me out after three years 'cause of my good behavior. I made nice with the bulls and told the warden that I could give him sure tips on the horsies once I got sprung."

"That's swell, Louie, and you're looking great." Once again I was telling a big one, since he looked like one of the decrepit nags he invariably advised people to bet on. "What are you doing to put bread on the table? I hope you're going straight this time."

"I swear to you, Mr. DeWitt, I swear on the grave of my sainted third uncle Padraic McNoodle that I'm going straight this time. But I'm not putting bread on the table these days. I put it on a plate. See, I learned good manners when I was in the pen. And as for a job, I started working last week at the Bank of Bulgaria over at 37th and Sixth. I'm a security guard."

"That's swell, Louie, and I'm real glad for you." I thought of standing him a drink but recalled the state of my tab. Besides, Gus was still mumbling.

Then I got a brainstorm. "Tell me, Louie, do you still see any of the old crowd, you know, all those guys who seemed to know everyone and anything that happens in this town?"

"Sure do, Mr. DeWitt." He beamed. "And I'd be glad to do you a favor if you need one. Just say the word. You always played fair with me."

Louie obviously didn't know that it was I who phoned in the anonymous tip that got him nabbed for safecracking and put in stir. I sometimes felt like a heel for doing it, but the reward was too good to pass up, especially if you were paying alimony and short of peanuts.

"Yeah, Louie, I could use a lead. Client of mine has got the hots for some broad, but she's gone AWOL and the trail's cold. She's about six-five, blonde, and has this thing for basketball. Ring a bell with you?"

"It doesn't even ring-a-ding with me, Mr. DeWitt, but I can ask around and let you know. You still living in that same dump you had? Got the same phone?"

I assured Louie that neither the dump nor my phone number had changed since he paid his respects to the slammer. "I could be in like Flynn if I find her, and I won't forget who helped me," I promised. "Here's my card. And Louie," I advised, "keep your nose clean this time."

"I sure will, Mr. DeWitt. I keep plenty of Kleenex with me. I'll be in touch."

We shook hands and Louie went back to a table where what looked like a pride of petty thieves had gathered. Poor Louie, I thought.

I had finished my drink long before. I looked at Gus. He sneered and gave me the finger. I shrugged and took a sip from a half-empty glass nearby. I was sorry I did that: Gin rickeys don't mate well with Black Russians. I got up to leave. Gertie blew me another kiss and I blew one back, hoping I didn't catch anything that I no ways wanted to catch. But she was a sweet gal at heart. So I threw her a handful of peanuts before calling it a night at The Slippery Elbow.

6

Sunday the dick slept late. I had a slight hangover from boozing it up the night before and fatigue from dealing with my client Mr. Baker, Chinaman Charlie, and Fatso at the museum. Chasing a bus hadn't helped either. Besides that— as if that weren't enough—my gut felt funny from all the Spam and peanuts I had consumed. Gotta learn that Spam and peanuts just don't mix.

When I finally crawled out of bed around 2:30, the day was half shot. By this hour people had returned home from church and fire-and-brimstone sermons. And, I thought, if they were among the lucky ones not out of work during this awful depression, they were well into their regular Sunday meal of chicken, mashed potatoes, peas, and chocolate cake.

I yawned, stretched, scratched myself, and headed for the john to take care of matters. I felt lousy and the mirror made things worse. A shower helped a little. So did brushing my teeth. The hell with rubbing the enamel off them, I told myself. The gut still bothered me, but I managed to get down a couple pieces of stale rye toast and some java. That was plenty for now.

I spent the rest of the afternoon reading the comics, the only part of the Sunday paper I enjoyed. Come to think of it, it was about the only worthwhile part of any day's paper.

How much news about people out of work and committing suicide or one lousy European country threatening another can you take? I know that somehow, some day, these stinking bad times will give way to better ones. Yeah, maybe some day. But some day when? At least I do know that we'll never get stuck in another war just to pull England's chestnuts out of the fire. Give me a steady diet of "Blondie," "Mutt and Jeff," and of course "Dick Tracy," from whom I learned most of my trade, and I'll be as happy as a pig in you-know-what.

Trouble was that a black cloud had drifted over me and was raining drops of doldrums on my head. I had the Sunday blues and not even listening to "Amos 'n' Andy" was helping. A shot of Jack Daniel's didn't do much for me either. Nor, I figured, would going to see the latest Garbo flick. Then the phone rang. Who'd call me on a Sunday, I wondered. Who'd call me at home any day?

"I got two words for you, wise guy," said the caller. "Butt out."

I thought real fast. This bozo, who spoke with an accent, can't be a friend. Raising my voice an octave, I answered, "To whom do you wish to speak, sir?" I figured the disguise would throw him for a loop.

"I want to speak to your Aunt Fanny about a certain matter."

Maybe the call was legit after all. I did have an Aunt Flora, but she had been sent to the Wisconsin Home for the Criminally Insane fifteen years earlier for dicing her husband, Mack, and then stuffing his ears with sauteed onions. Maybe this guy did know Flora and had got her name wrong. One way or another I was determined to find out.

"I'm so sorry, but dear Aunt Fanny has gone out for the evening to play mah-jongg with her friends. Would you be so kind as to leave your name and number? It would also be of great assistance if you would elaborate on 'butt out'." That should do it, I thought.

"Listen, you damn pansy, you're getting my goat. I want you to stop looking for you-know-who or you'll be looking for what's between your legs."

Puzzled as I was, the more I thought about the strange caller and stranger message, the more the pieces didn't seem to fit. I had a case now, strange as it was. Forget it, I told myself. Stop thinking about the threats, or you'll lose sight of finding Mona. Maybe she'll turn up tomorrow. Sure, sure. Like maybe I don't know on what side of the toast I slap my margarine.

It had been a short, hard day, and I had nothing to show for it except a few guffaws from the funny papers. I looked out my filthy windows. It seemed to be raining again.

7

Monday was another day, another week. But for some reason I didn't have the old Monday workday blues. Maybe it was because I had had the Sunday blues. Maybe it was because I almost never had any work to do on Mondays. And maybe, just maybe, it was because I had a good feeling about finding Mona.

I walked up the stairs to my office cheerfully whistling "Brother, Can You Spare a Dime?" En route I read the riot act to a vagrant who was sleeping in the stairwell. The sight of that scruffy guy nearly broke my good mood.

Dotty was ferreting through the file cabinet when I opened the door at 10:18. She was either cleaning dustballs or looking for the remains of an old sandwich that one of us might have left. As far as I could tell, it had been a long time since the cabinet had housed anything serious. "Morning, babe. Get lucky over the weekend?"

"As a matter of fact I did, although I'm not sure if that's any of your business," she huffed. "They were running a special on melons at the grocery store, and you know how hard it is to get good melons this time of year."

My Gal Friday could be a bit slow, even downright stupid, if you ask me, but she had her melons, I have to say. I also have to say that they looked real swell lurking there inside her red angora sweater.

"Good for you, kid." I took off my coat and hat, sat at my desk, put my feet up, and asked the usual: "Any messages?"

"Yeah. There was a certain Mr. Baker who called, but he didn't leave his name."

I almost jumped out of my chair. "Whaddya mean he didn't leave his name? Didn't you say the call came from a Mr. Baker?"

Dopey Dotty thought for a minute. "I guess I should have said that he didn't leave his first name," she giggled.

I felt like sending her down to play with the vagrant. "Did he leave a message?"

"Ah . . . yeah. He said to call him."

That would have been fine except, of course, I hadn't got around to finding out where or how I could reach him when he was here on Saturday. I guess Dotty might not be the only dopey one.

I was stewing in my juices while anxiously waiting for Mr. Baker to call back. Dotty watered the artificial plant, then returned to reading *War and Peace*. She had finished the complete works of Dickens. Meanwhile the phone remained as silent as I wish my ex-wife had been throughout most of our marriage. We didn't have a clock on the wall, but tick, tock, tick, tock was in my brain.

I had had enough of sitting there waiting for the damn contraption to ring. Dotty was laughing hysterically, probably over the part where Napoleon invades Russia and all those soldiers get slaughtered. She was getting on my nerves.

Then it struck me, a bolt right out of the blue, or in today's case, the gray. I didn't know Baker's first name, but why not look up "Baker" in the phone book and see if my man's listed? They don't call me Super Sleuth for nothing. (I have been called a few other names.)

"Hey, Dotty, put down that crap and go get our telephone directory. Look up 'Baker' and start calling each one to see if you can find our client."

Dotty looked pissed, as only Dotty can look pissed. "Do I have to? I had my nails manicured Friday and I don't want to spoil them," she whined and began picking at what remained of her cuticles.

"Listen, Dotty, you're not getting paid to just sit around and look like Harlow, you know."

"Oh, all right. But just remember that I'm not getting paid at all these days."

She had a point. I went back to stewing in my juices, and Dotty got out the directory. She turned the pages and continued to pick at her cuticles. At least ten minutes passed. Then she looked up with a sort of pained expression and asked, "How do you spell 'Baker'?" There are days it doesn't pay to get out of bed, I thought.

Somehow she managed to process the information. "There are a lot of 'Bakers,' you know. Do I have to call all of them?"

"No," I said, "only those with telephone numbers."

"But they all have telephone numbers or they wouldn't be listed. Isn't that so?"

"Yes, Dotty," I sighed. "Start with the first one and then keep phoning until you get the right one."

"But what happens if I don't get the right one, Mr. D?"

I gave serious thought to firing her on the spot, but a glance at her melons, platinum hair, and come-hither, gap-toothed mouth told me to cool it. But I had to get out of the place.

"I'm going to Ma's for some hash," I informed her. "Want me to bring you back something, or are you eating out?"

"Bring me back something from Ma's. I'm dieting, so it should be something light. Let me think.''

Letting her think, I feared, was going to delay my lunchtime until supper. "I know. Bring me back a tongue and limburger cheese sandwich on white bread with lots and lots of mayo. Oh, and an extra portion of French fries. But skip the dessert today because it's fattening." There was something seriously wrong with this dame.

Once at Ma's, I caught Betty's eye. She gave me her usual nasty look and sauntered over. She was still sore either about the tip she thought I had swiped or because I had left her only a nickel on Friday.

"Yeah, whatta you want today, big sport?"

"I'll have a cuppa split pea soup and a BLT."

She smirked. "How do you want your pee split? And what's a BLT? Both Little Testicles?"

I wanted to split something for her, namely her lip, but settled for warning her that she'd get no tip if she continued to speak that way to me.

"Honey, if I had to depend on people like you for tips, I might as well be walking the streets."

I let it go at that. I wasn't sure what she meant by "walking the streets," although I could see her walking a dog, preferably a pit bull that would make her cry "uncle" even if she didn't have one.

I wolfed down my lunch. I wanted to finish the foul-smelling and worse-tasting soup and sandwich as quickly as possible so that I could get back to the office and see what Dopey Dotty had come up with. Betty the Beast brought me the check along with the eats I was picking up for Dotty. I left Betty a bigger tip this time: a dime. I didn't bother to let her know that the dime was lying on the counter next to me when I sat down.

This time I took the elevator up to my office, fearful that Ma's fine cooking was about to come up on me any minute. I handed Dotty her food. She immediately dumped one of the containers of fries on her tongue and cheese sandwich. Then she took the ketchup and mixed it with the mayo that covered the bread.

"Dotty, if you can stop for a moment making like Chef Boyardee, could you tell me if you were able to get in touch with Baker."

"I got in touch with all the Bakers that were in the white pages, Mr. D, but no luck. Want me to look in the Yellow Pages and call all those bakers too?"

"No, you did well, babe." There I went lying again. "Wait a minute," I whooped.

"But Mr. D, I'm so hungry!"

"No, no. I just got an idea that might work. I did some work for a dame a few years back, and she owes me a favor or two. Just so happens that she works for Ma Bell and might be able to see if there's any 'Baker' with an unlisted number."

"But Mr. D, don't you need to have the number if you want to phone your client?"

"Bite your tongue, Dotty," I advised, hoping that she would take me literally.

I dialed the operator and asked for Sadie Plotz. Sadie seemed pleased when she came on the phone and learned that it was yours truly.

"Dick DeWitt! How sweet of you to call! I'm busy this Saturday but I'm free tonight, Tuesday, Wednesday, Thursday, Friday, and Sunday. Which is best for you?"

Despite playing hard to get, Sadie had this thing for me. Sadie, in fact, had a thing for anyone who fit the general description of male. I first knew her when she hired me to check up on her hubby, who, she was convinced, was breaking their holy vows of marital fidelity. She explained this to me as we were having some hanky-panky on her foyer floor a few minutes after we walked into her apartment. I never did find out more about hubby, probably because Sadie took up most of my time and energy doing the horizontal rumba. She was disappointed that I couldn't learn anything about her spouse but told me that she enjoyed dancing with me more than going to Roseland. We might still be dancing if her husband hadn't caught her doing the one-step, two-step with some Mexican chihuahua who had tickled her tostadas. After the husband turned the wetback into a hairless chihuahua I was taking no chances.

I apologized to Sadie that I couldn't see her for the time being since J. Edgar Hoover had asked for my help in tracking down a gang of desperados who had escaped from Alcatraz by stealing the warden's hot air balloon. I promised that once my mission was accomplished I would come over to her place and practice the latest dances. Meanwhile I asked her if she could do me a big one and see if there was an unlisted phone for any "Baker."

"For my favorite dick I'd do anything," she trilled. "Hang on." A few minutes later a chastened Sadie returned to the line and informed me that there was no such unlisted number. "But don't be a stranger," she added. "Come up and see me some time."

I had struck out again. It was now 3:30. I told Dotty, who had finished *War and Peace* and was halfway through *The Odyssey*, to take the rest of the day off and go home and see to her melons. She said they weren't ripe yet. I said that was a matter of opinion and told her to scram. I hung around until 5:30 in case Baker should call again. Nothing. Or almost nothing. I figured out what I had done wrong playing cat's cradle last week.

8

I was in a sour mood and ready to spit nails when I reached the office the next morning. I had returned home yesterday to find a nasty note taped to my door courtesy of the landlord. I didn't mind being told that my rent was long overdue, but I did take offense at being labeled a "deadbeat."

Dotty was reading again when I walked in. This time it was Proust.

"What happened to *The Odyssey*?" I asked.

"Oh, I finished that when I got here this morning."

"So fast?"

"Well, I sort of skipped over all the parts that had this man Odysseus in it. I wanted to find out about this other guy Homer, but the author never talked about him. Anyhow, it was all Greek to me."

Just keep your eyes on those melons and it will be all right, I counseled myself. I asked Miss Einstein if anyone had called but didn't get a reply. She was too absorbed in Proust.

With nothing to do, my mind drifted to my constant problem: money. My landlord was getting antsier than ever, and the rent for my office would be coming up shortly. And no Mr. Baker. And no other client. I was getting so desperate that I called Harry the Shyster, a lawyer who had employed me on a job about six, seven months ago.

"Hello, Harry, this is your old pal Dick DeWitt."

"Well, well, look who showed up from under the rocks this morning. What do you want, you stupid, incompetent bastard?"

I took this to mean that Harry was in a worse mood than I was and that I had better softsoap him if I was going to get anywhere. "Just thought I'd give a friendly call and see how you and the family were doing."

"Not that it's any concern of yours, but my mother-in-law has been staying with us for five weeks, my son has been smoking reefers, and my daughter has run off with a grease monkey. Now tell me what you want, you creep, and be quick about it."

"Harry, I know that we had a mild difference of opinion over the last job, but I sure could use some work just now."

There was a slight pause before Vesuvius erupted. "A 'mild' difference? The state nearly took away my license because of what you did! I should have called my friends whose names end with a vowel to play stickball with your gonads."

He was having difficulty breathing, and I feared that he would have a seizure before he could hire me. "Come on now, Harry, the district attorney was none too happy with me either. Let's let bygones be bygones," I said in my most poetic manner.

"DeWitt, if you ever call me again, I'll personally see to it that you won't have any fingers to ever call anyone else. I wouldn't hire you if you were the last gumshoe on the planet."

The phone went dead. I figured it was useless to call back and explain that by no means was I the last gumshoe on the planet.

I sat there cracking my knuckles and wondering whether I should take a stroll around the block and buy some peanuts. I could send Dotty for the peanuts, I thought, but she looked so contented mouthing Proust that I didn't have the heart to interrupt her. Besides, the last time I sent her out for peanuts she came back with a bagful of empty shells. I shook her by the shoulders but couldn't get her to admit that she had devoured the peanuts. She said that the empty shells came that way. I half believed her.

I had about made up my mind to take that stroll when the phone rang. It was Light Fingers Louie.

"I got some news for you, Mr. DeWitt. Meet me tonight at The Slippery Elbow any time after 9:00 and I'll let you have it. I think you'll be real pleased."

"That's great, Louie, but why can't you tell me now? Are you being followed?"

"Nah, but I got a tickle in my throat and have to go get some cough drops. Until later, Mr. DeWitt."

Click. The stupid sonofabitch had hung up before I could press him to give with the details. I'd like to tickle his you-know-what with those cough drops. Well, I thought, at least I'm getting somewhere.

The rest of the day proved uneventful. Dotty had put down the Proust for the time being and had immersed herself in trying to solve Fermat's last theorem. I wasn't much hungry but went out and bought a bag of peanuts to go with the two hardboiled eggs I had brought from home. Afterwards I lollygagged, dozing and waking on the office couch. I asked Dotty if she would like to join me there, but she said it had room only for one and besides, she hadn't finished solving her Fermat yet. Meanwhile Mr. Baker continued on the lam. He was making me mad.

I fixed a light supper when I got home. Some canned stew and four strawberry cupcakes, which I washed down with a root beer. I would have preferred something stronger to drink but needed to keep a clear head for my rendezvous with Louie.

Something told me that tonight at the Elbow would be different. Events proved me right. The first thing that greeted me when I pushed through the doors promptly at 9:00 was the sight of some guy lying on top of Gardenia Gertie. Gertie was acting fast, fast even for Gertie, I thought, and getting right down to business. I went over and clubbed the guy repeatedly with my blackjack. Big mistake. Gertie explained that the two of them had been doing the turkey trot when they slipped on the wet floor. I bought that, even though the joint never played any music. I told Gus the barman to give the poor putz a drink when he came to and put it on my tab. Gus seemed none too pleased.

"Hey, Mr. DeWitt, over here," came a voice sotto voce.

"Hiya, Louie," I said. "You got something for me?"

"Sure do, Mr. DeWitt." Louie looked nervously about the room to make sure no one was eavesdropping. "I did some calling, mostly to guys I knew in the Big House but also to a couple of politicians who had employed my expertise for various capers, if you know what I mean."

"I know what you mean, Louie. Now just get on with it."

"Okay, okay. At first—nothing. Then Florsheim Al called. You know him, he's the mug with a brogue who's got this thing for shoes and did time in the jug for separating a judge's wife from her front teeth when she accidentally scuffed his brand-new wingtips. Anyways, he tells me that he might have seen this Mona playing basketball with two little kids over at 65th and West End. She was beating the hell out of them too. Gave each of them a black eye for scoring a basket against her. She seemed like one tough cookie to him." Louie took a few gulps from his Pabst Blue Ribbon and wiped the foam off his lips. "But there's more. This Al likes his dames tough, and so he decides to follow her and see where she lives. Unfortunately, she went directly to the YWCA three blocks north and got into an elevator. Stymied, he goes to the front desk and asks for her name, but the guy at the desk threatens to throw him out on his keester. Al would have shown him right then and there who was boss, but he was wearing freshly shined shoes."

"Louie, I got to hand it to you. You did good," I told him. "Here, let me treat you to some hooch. I'll tell Gus to send it over. And Louie, don't forget to let me know if you hear anything more."

I always said Louie was a good yegg and this proved it. I could almost smell Mona from here, despite the total lack of ventilation in the place. Tomorrow I'd visit the Y for myself. Meanwhile I told Gus to fix Louie a cheap one and put it on the tab. I smiled at Gertie as I was leaving, but she was on her back again with some Johnny on top. They must have slipped again. Outside it wasn't raining.

9

I got up earlier than usual the next morning, performed my ablutions, and got cleaned up. A quick cup of coffee and a couple of jelly donuts and I was off to the Y. I was dressed snappily: clean shirt, mostly clean tie, jacket and trousers that more or less matched, and a beret that I had recently had blocked at my local hatter's. The sun hadn't bothered to show up yet, but I put on my sunglasses, since all self-respecting dicks are supposed to wear them while tailing someone.

The bus got me to the Y in pretty good time, considering the rush-hour traffic. I did miss my stop because I was wearing the Foster Grant specs, but not by much. Once inside I cased the place. It was filled with broads. I made a mental note to hang out here some lonely Saturday night and get the lay of the land, if you catch my drift.

The guy at the information desk was checking me out. His pursed lips and the pink rose in the lapel buttonhole of his jacket clued me in that his interest in the Y's inhabitants was purely professional.

"Thomething that I can help you with?" he lisped. He gave me the biggest smile I had seen since my ex-wife had learned that I had developed a hernia.

"Yeah, maybe there is. I'm looking for someone very tall and blonde," I told him.

"Oh my, aren't we all?" he purred and fluttered his false eyelashes. "Do you have a name?"

I wasn't going to give my legal name. I was too smart for that. "Richard DeWitt," I said. That should throw him off the track.

"No, thir," he giggled. "I mean do you have a name for the young lady?"

This guy was sharp. "Yeah, her first name is Mona but I forgot her last one."

"I'm tharry, but the only Mona who hangths her panty girdle here and callth it home—the place not her girdle, mind you—is average height—thay about four-eleven—and bald. Until a few months ago when she moved out we did have thomeone who fitth your general dethcription. Her name was Petunia Pettigrew. I ethspecially remember her becuth she always was carrying a bathketball. She theemed like a thweet girl, but she was forced to leave after dribbling the ball on another girl'th head."

No cigar, but I could tell I was getting warm. I took off my coat. "Any forwarding address for this Pettigrew gal?"

He drew himself up to his full height, which wasn't much. "Thir, I'm not allowed to give out thuch information."

No problem, I thought. A promise to send him some fresh pink roses and to stop by and pick him up for dinner some night next week loosened his tongue. He suggested a dimly lit Hungarian restaurant he frequented, where "thimply gorgeous" Gypsy men played violins, came to your table, and whispered "Was there anything thpecial you'd like?" I made a mental note to go there by myself and ask the strolling Gypsy to make my goulash hot with a lot of paprika. Meanwhile this guy at the desk was promising the addresses of all the girls. I said Petunia's would do fine.

I had Petunia's address now and hoped that she'd turn out to be Mona living under a different name, a nom de plum as the Frenchies say. Trouble was that Petunia/Mona lived outside the city limits. Cab fare would cost me my liver,

39

which, smothered with onions, I was looking forward to cooking tonight. Then I remembered that I knew someone who drove a taxi for a living. This someone owed me.

I first met William "Dilly" (aka "Willy Dilly") Farkas a year ago when we were retching in the men's room after having polished off one of Ma's blue plate specials, which for some reason included part of the blue plate itself. We went to a nearby bar afterwards and got to know each other pretty well. Dilly had done all sorts of odd jobs, including taming armadillos, for which he got good pay. He had also paid dearly for once lifting a skirt. Unfortunately for him, someone had been wearing the skirt at the time. Even more unfortunate, she was a he. When Dilly got out of traction three months later, he decided to mend his ways and settle down to a more normal life. But he didn't know what to do. I told him that I had an "in" with some mug who owned a few taxis and that I could get him a job if he could hack it. I got him the job and his promise that if I ever needed help I should call him. I had meant to keep in touch with Dilly, especially since I was curious to hear more about his intimate relations with armadillos. But I hadn't. This morning was a different story: I needed a freebie in the form of a ride to Petunia's.

I called Dilly and reached his wife, Amaryllis. I had never met her but Dilly had shown me her photo the night we were chasing down a few beers. I seemed to recall that with her long nose and bony body she bore a faint resemblance to an armadillo. Funny how things like that stick in your mind.

"Hello, Mrs. Farkas, this is Dick DeWitt, a pal of your husband's. Is he around by any chance."

There was a pause. "By some chance the lousy, two-timing, four-flusher, rat bastard, no-good-for-nothing, cheat, liar is still in bed. Hang on and I'll get the shithead, lowlife scumbag for you."

I got the feeling that something was wrong with Dilly's marriage but decided to keep my trap shut.

"Hey, Mr. DeWitt, what gives?" a voice still groggy with sleep got on the line.

I explained to Dilly what favor I needed. He said he'd pick me up in front of the Y in half an hour. He was off work today but had no desire to stay home and listen to that skinny, ugly, filthy whore of a foul-mouthed wife of his. I guessed he didn't like her too much either.

Good as his word, Dilly arrived right on time with his Checker Cab. He was wearing a yellow and black checkered jacket to match the cab. He wasn't wearing any trousers, however. I guessed he had been in a hurry to leave home.

Dilly took the long way around either to avoid traffic or because he didn't know the direct way. This part of the city looked even dingier than the part I knew best. But it was my city, and I loved it. Warts and all, although I had to admit that the only warts I'd seen recently had been those on the nose of Mrs. Heidegger, the busybody who lived down the hall from me and who liked to corner me and ask if I'd heard any juicy gossip.

The ride was uneventful save when Dilly tried, unsuccessfully, to run down a mean-looking dog. He said it reminded him of his wife.

At last we reached Hooker Avenue, where Petunia supposedly was living. It seemed crowded for this time of day, but the people, almost all of them females, were friendly as hell. When the cab pulled over, several women sporting exceptionally little clothing for this late in the year came over to ask if we'd like to have a good time. You don't get this kind of friendliness from everyone, I thought, but I had to see about Petunia. I told Dilly to wait for me. He seemed perfectly content with that, especially since one of the women said she could help him keep his legs warm.

The house was big as a mansion but needed a paint job almost as much as I needed a paycheck. A stately oak tree glumly stood guard over a series of unpruned bushes in the spacious front yard, which was overgrown with dead weeds. I nearly tripped over the broken sidewalk as I looked back at one of the women who was loudly insisting to Dilly that life was short but she could bet that he was long.

I knocked on the door. No one answered. I thought of throwing a loose piece of the sidewalk through the front window but settled for kicking the door repeatedly. A bleached-blonde crone with lipstick applied at a forty-five-degree angle answered and said she was sore and couldn't give any more today. I couldn't figure out why she was mad, but I was touched that this generous soul had given to charitable causes.

I asked her if Petunia was on the premises. She growled that she had sent her packing two days ago. "My lady friends and their gents couldn't take any more of her and her basketball." She told me that when she met Petunia and asked her if she knew how to score, Petunia said she was the best. "I didn't know the bitch was talking about basketball," the crone complained. "I don't run that kind of establishment, you know." As it turned out, Petunia had left no forwarding address. I was back to the starting gate.

Dilly looked a little the worse for wear but had a big smile on his face. "Haven't felt this good since I beat the crap out of the missus," he bragged. You could always count on Dilly to give you a laugh or two.

We stopped on our way back to the city for lunch at a dingy-looking diner. Before we went in, Dilly took a soiled, Indian-design blanket from the trunk and wrapped it around himself to compensate for his lack of trousers. The spoon at Archimedes' Pantheon was so greasy, so to speak, that it slipped from your fingers and had to be held with two hands. Dilly had the Archimedes special, a cheeseburger but without the cheese. I told the tired-looking hag who served us that I wanted a BLT, but hold the mayo. "Hold it yourself, lard ass," she replied, "and tell your friend Tonto to do the same." This broad must be the sister of Betty the waitress at Ma's, I thought.

Afterwards Dilly insisted on driving me directly to my office. I had taken him at his word when he said that he'd be glad to do me a favor anytime. I didn't offer to pay any fare, but I did slip him a George Washington. He merited it. "See you around, Dilly," I said and waved good-bye. I didn't catch what he said, but it sounded like "luck you." I guess the whole sentence was "Good luck to you."

I was too tired to climb the eight floors to my office. I pressed the elevator button and waited for Joe to bring the conveyance down. Fifteen minutes later they both appeared. Since no one else was in the elevator, I concluded that Joe was off the wagon again. When he hiccupped "hello," his breath smelled like an army of skunks had bivouacked in his mouth overnight.

Dotty was reading and chewing on her fingernails when I opened the door. I guess that Proust was telling a good ghost story.

"Any calls, babe?"

"Which day are you talking about, Mr. D?"

I told her to go back to Proust but stay in the office until 5:00 in case someone did call and if someone did, to call me at home.

"You got it, Mr. D."

You got it too, Dotty, I thought, but exactly what sure beats me.

10

Slow night. No call from Dotty. No call from anyone. I heated up the leftover canned stew, gobbled down a couple of cupcakes, and called it a meal for want of a better word. Nothing much on the radio, so I headed to the Elbow for a few quick ones and a friendly face or two.

You would have thought that they were holding a wake, and not an Irish one, at the joint. It was quiet as the city morgue, and only a solitary rummy sat there getting misty-eyed over the pair of deuces life had dealt him. Even Gertie wasn't there. This must be her night for the opera, Gus said. I had a Cuba Libre, thought better of a second one, and went home.

Next morning when I got to the office Dotty was all hepped up. I figured that Proust had been giving her a thrill, but it turned out that someone had called and left a message.

"It's him, it's him! It's Mr. Baker! He left his number and said for you to call him as soon as you got in." She was getting her good-sized knockers in an uproar.

It was enough to give a guy religion. The call and also her good-sized knockers. I dialed the number before I even took off my galoshes, which I had put on because the radio predicted the possibility of the season's first snow flurries.

"Hello?" came a frightened voice.

"Hello, Mr. Baker, this is Dick DeWitt. Where've you been?"

"I've been running, Mr. DeWitt, running scared. Some-one called me at home on Sunday and said I was going to be sorry that I went to you for help. He was real nasty. Said that you were so dumb you couldn't tell excrement from a certain brand of shoe polish but that he wasn't going to take any chances, and that we'd better call off the hunt for a certain lady or else."

I was boiling mad. I didn't mind this goon's threats, but I did mind the insult to my intelligence: I definitely knew the difference between excrement and that shoe polish. I had known it for some time now.

"Listen, Mr. Baker. Come over to my office and we'll sort things out. I'm going to find Mona for you, don't you worry."

"Oh, I hope so, Mr. DeWitt. I can't imagine what life without her would be like."

I felt sorry for this poor sap and for all saps who let a screwy dame putty their brains. "Don't you worry," I said. "Just come over."

"I can't. I'm afraid. Someone's been following me. Can you meet me in a public place? That way I'd feel a lot safer."

I didn't want to leave the office and meet him. For one thing, how could I be sure that this mug who was threatening us wouldn't put some lead into me as soon as I walked outside. More important, my feet were sore as hell. Years of trailing up and down streets and alleyways were catching up with me. But a dick's a dick, and he's gotta do what a dick does do. And what a dick does do . . . ah, forget it, I thought.

"Sure, Mr. Baker, I'll be glad to meet you. Where will it be?"

"Can you meet me at Le Grand Rien, that fancy French hotel that opened a couple of months ago? I'm calling from a phone booth not far away."

"You got it. I'll be there in less than thirty minutes."

I took a couple of sips of Dotty's freshly brewed coffee and was sorry. Very sorry. I thought of Socrates and his cup

45

of hemlock. Then I pocketed my .38 and told my book-besotted, mocha-making menace that I'd be back sometime in the afternoon. She nodded her head vaguely. She had returned to reading Proust. Her knockers had calmed down.

Once outside the building I searched for suspicious-looking characters who might tail me. There was an extremely small man sitting astride a huge Great Dane and prodding it to go down the block, but that didn't worry me. In this city you see everything. Besides, this jockey and his canine mount were moving too slowly to catch anything, including a cold.

I was in a hurry to see my client, so I hailed a bus rather than walk and got to our rendezvous only fifteen minutes late.

I had not seen the Le Grand Rien before. The sight of it nearly knocked the white socks off my feet. It was big and then some. A doorman wearing some faggot-looking wig and dressed like he was going to a Halloween party greeted me in what I took to be Frenchie language and held open the door. If he thought that was going to earn him a tip, he was crazier than he looked. The inside of the hotel almost knocked my socks off a second time. There were more of these characters wearing their goofy-looking Halloween costumes than Carter has liver pills. What the hell are they doing here, I wondered, making a movie of the French Revolution? I lost my head for a moment, thinking of myself starring in the movie as King Louie. You know, the guy who came from that family that had all that Bourbon.

"Call for Mr. DeWitt, call for Mr. DeWitt."

A sawed-off bellboy who looked like he was peddling Philip Morris cigarettes was casing the lobby like there was no tomorrow.

"Over here, shorty," I called. Mindful that this might be a trap, I patted him down to make sure that he wasn't packing a rod. Can't be too careful, I thought, not with all the sinister things that had been happening.

"Please, sir, that tickles. If you want to do that again, I suggest that you wait until I'm off work."

I told him I couldn't wait that long. I asked why he was trying to wake the dead by screaming out my name for all the world to hear and told him that if he did that one more time I was going to reduce him in size from dwarf to midget. That calmed him down. He told me to go to the registration desk and pick up the house phone. Someone wanted to speak with me. He said that he didn't know who. I tipped him with a thank-you.

Gumshoes—at least the best of them, like myself—know when they're being set up. I walked nonchalantly to the registration desk, gave the man behind the counter a "none-of-your-lip" look, and picked up the phone. "Listen, you filthy swine, I'm going to get Mona back for her Casper Milquetoast and you're going to watch your toenails grow real long in the slammer. You got that?"

"Mr. DeWitt, it's me, Uneeda Baker. I'm sitting near the entrance to the Chateau Marquis de Sade Restaurant. I'm right behind a woman who's wearing a large hat and flossing her teeth."

"Gotcha, Mr. B." I hung up and headed his way. Good things were breaking fast. Now I had a first name for my client and the name of a good French restaurant, where, if I ever get paid, I might take some broad to chow down and exchange a few parlay-vouses with.

My client appeared haggard. He looked like Lucky Lindy must have when he finished flying the Atlantic. The bags under his eyes were sagging so much that I thought he was carrying a change of clothes in them.

"Mr. Baker," I said, "you look like you were traveling on the *Titanic* but forgot to get off when it hit the iceberg." I thought that might give him a chuckle.

"Please don't joke, Mr. DeWitt. I feel awful. Some guy is threatening me and, worst of all, I don't have my Mona."

He started to cry, real hard like. I handed him my handkerchief, which was mostly clean, and told him to wipe the snot that was dribbling from his nose and to act like a man, or at least a mature woman. I felt like slapping some sense into him and also for dropping so much snot into my handkerchief. I usually change the latter every three months or so, but I had started this one only last week and it hadn't seen much action until now.

"Come on, Mr. Baker. Get a hold of yourself. I told you I'd find Mona, and I will. So perk up. You gotta have faith."

He stopped blubbering, blew some more into my handkerchief, and gave me a weak smile. "I do have faith, Mr. DeWitt. I was raised as a Pentecostal and handled snakes until I lost control of one in church one Sunday. The critter slithered from my neck and finished off my Aunt Mildred, who had been standing next to me, clapping her hands and singing 'Swanee.' I guess the snake would have preferred Al Jolson's version." He dried his eyes with my handkerchief before handing it to me. I let it drop to the floor. "Now I'm a God-fearing Holy Roller," he continued, "and I read the Good Book whenever I can." He paused. "I still like to go to zoos and watch snakes, but I learned my lesson and don't play with them when someone's standing next to me." He blew his nose hard. I wished he had kept the handkerchief. Then he asked what I had learned so far about his beloved.

I was tempted to ask, in return, what a dame like Mona, who sounded perfectly normal, was doing with a guy like him, but my empty billfold screamed don't do it. "I've learned this and that, as well as these and those," I told him, "but I'd rather play it close to my hairy chest until I have a few more chickens set up in a row like clay pigeons." I figured I'd let him try to parse that sentence while I concocted a big whopper to conceal the fact that I had learned zippo.

He stood there scratching his head for the longest time. I dodged the flakes of dandruff that were attacking me like the Red Baron flying his Fokker and spitting bullets. I was having enough trouble trying to find Mona and nab the Fokker who had kidnapped her.

"Let's cut to the quick, Uneeda, if I may be so familiar as to call you by your Christian Pentecostal Holy Roller name rather than adhere to the strict formality of employing your surname," I said. That at least got him to stop scratching. "I could use more information about her, even if you don't think it's important. Think. Did you ever meet any of her friends or relatives? Did she have any interests other than basketball, art, and Chinese food?"

"Come to think of it, she does have a girlfriend who she used to talk a lot about. Let me see . . . Abigail . . . Abigail Snerd, that's her name."

"Was she related to Mortimer Snerd?" I asked, only joshing, of course.

"No, but she was a distant relation of the golfer Sammy Snead. They misspelled her name at the hospital when she was born. It was supposed to be "A-b-i-g-a-l-e Snerd.""

As they say, you should quit while you're ahead.

But I wasn't about to quit. First of all, I wasn't "ahead" in any way, shape, or form. And second, I hadn't received a red cent for any of the legwork I had done. I approached the matter of payment gingerly. "Uneeda, if you expect me to go on looking for Mona, especially before someone takes it into his head to slit her throat, I'll need some bread."

I could have bitten my tongue as soon as the word came out. My client proceeded to list every damn kind of bread he could bake, informing me that I was welcome to as many loaves as the case needed. I sighed and explained what I had meant.

"Oh, that's no problem, Mr. DeWitt." He took some bills out of his wallet and peeled off two C-notes. "Here, take them," he said. "There's more if you need it."

I'm not sure how wide my mouth gaped, but I figure that Jonah's whale could have entered. Cripes! Two big ones! I was about to plant a couple of smackers on Baker's balding head, but this didn't seem the right time or place.

"These will do just fine for now. I can use them to grease a few palms and pry open a couple of mouths," I told him. What I didn't tell him was that the palms were mine and that the mouth that needed attention was also mine. I was getting sick of leftover canned stew and cupcakes for dinner.

I told Baker that I'd be on the case day and night and would be in touch. Meanwhile, he should look after himself and call me with any news. We shook hands and were about to go our separate ways when we heard: "Calling Mr. DeWitt. Calling Mr. DeWitt." I thought it was a long-lost echo, but then I caught sight of the Johnny-from-Philip Morris look-alike.

"Here, Rumpelstiltskin, and don't take all day about it," I hollered across the lobby.

He didn't seem too pleased but sauntered over and handed me a note. He hung around waiting for something, probably a tip, but I told him to scram. I could read the note without any help from him.

The note read: "You can't escape me. You're being watched." It was signed: "The Black Llama." I wheeled around but couldn't see any black llama in the place. Not even a purple cow. I showed the note to my client. He turned ashen. I could tell it had ruined his day. It wasn't doing much for mine either.

11

How could I have missed seeing a black llama? I gave a quick thought to spending some of the spondulicks that Baker had given me on consulting an eye doctor. I gave more serious thought to lunch since it was now 12:45 and my stomach was making as much noise as the alums at a Harvard-Yale football game. I could have splurged and had a tunafish sandwich with a side order of spareribs and sauerkraut right there at the Chateau Marquis de Sade Restaurant but settled for something less pretentious at a chophouse a block away from the hotel.

I got back to the office around 2:00 and found a note from Dotty. Since business was slow, it ran, she was taking the p.m. off to attend a lecture on the relative merits of Einstein's theory of relativity and Heisenberg's uncertainty principle. I hoped that she hadn't forgotten to take along her Proust to read while the speaker paused between sentences.

I spent the rest of the afternoon doing odds and ends, but mostly odds. I walked down the stairs and told Joe the elevator man that no one had yet fixed the sign on my office door and that I expected better treatment from the owner of this two-bit flophouse. After I walked back up I sat around totaling my IOUs to various creditors. I wouldn't have much change left over from my advance if I were to pay them off all at once. That gave me a good horse laugh. I only serve who stand and wait, to paraphrase the English poet Milton somebody or other. Then I counted the days to the holidays: Christmas, New Year's, Ground-hog Day. I made a note to send a few cards and a gift or two for each of those special occasions.

I was wondering what other pressing business I could take care of before calling it a day, when I suddenly remembered that Baker had given me the name of one of Mona's friends. I thumbed through the telephone book and found Abigail Snerd's number and address.

A sultry voice answered after a couple of rings. "Hello? Can I help you in any way? Are you in need of assistance? And who are you?"

This woman knew all the right questions to ask. I told her that I was working for Uneeda Baker, who was looking for his girlfriend Mona, and that he had mentioned her as a friend of Mona's.

"Mona? Sure I'm a friend of Mona's. A good one, too. I've been wondering where she's been keeping herself lately. I haven't seen her in a while. I know . . . why don't you come over to my place tonight, say about 8:30 or so, and we can talk about her. I'll put up some coffee and make some fudge brownies."

I didn't have to be asked twice. I didn't feel like going home to change and so I put on a spare shirt, the one that doesn't smell too bad and that I keep in the office for special occasions. I waited around for an hour or so and then put on my galoshes and left. It wasn't snowing yet but you could never tell. I had a quick, light meal at Ma's—a cup of Navy bean soup, a tossed salad, a loin of pork, mashed potatoes, a side order of succotash, three rolls with butter, and a dish of Jello. "Skip the whipped cream on the Jello," I ordered Betty, who had cleaned the counter and was now paring her nails on it. I wanted to leave room for Miss Snerd's fudge brownies. Feeling flush as John D. Rockefeller, I left a dime tip. My favorite waitress asked if it was real but pocketed it anyway. Miserable ingrate.

It wasn't snowing when I left Ma's. In fact, it was a beautiful clear, crisp night. I took off my galoshes and walked to my appointment with Abigail Snerd.

"Won't you come in?" she said as she opened the door.

Trained to observe the slightest detail, I noticed that she was wearing red see-through lounging pajamas. "I hope I haven't disturbed your sleep," I apologized, handing her my hat, coat, and galoshes.

"Not at all, Mr. DeWitt, but watch your step. Don't trip over Cuddles."

"Cuddles" was some sort of oversized jungle cat who didn't seem a bit pleased to make my acquaintance.

"Down, baby," Miss Snerd told the beast. "Let go of the nice man's tie."

The creature immediately stopped chewing my tie and grabbed the galoshes from his owner's hand. Got to say that for Cuddles: he's obedient.

Mona's friend lived in a really posh place. She led me down a few steps into a living room decorated with furniture that would make your eyes bigger than Eddie Cantor's. The drapes were open, giving a full view of the river below and the moon above. I concluded that Mona's friend was not spending her time frequenting soup kitchens or standing in bread lines.

I sat on her living room sofa and immediately sank in about a foot. The velvet cushions were that soft. "Why don't you come over here, Mr. DeWitt, and sit next to me on this tiger-skin love seat?" she asked as she patted it caressingly. "I think you'll find it ever so comfortable, and we can get much better acquainted."

I thanked her but said that I'd prefer to remain where I was. I hadn't sat on velvet cushions for years, I explained, and besides, I was allergic to tigers. I uttered the latter explanation in a whisper, for fear that Cuddles would take offense as well as my life.

She seemed disappointed. "Don't you want some, Mr. Private Investigator?"

"Of course I do." Her deep blue eyes lit up. "I've been thinking of those fudge brownies ever since we spoke on the telephone," I confessed.

Maybe the brownies hadn't turned out well or maybe she was plain tired. After all, she was in her pajamas. In any event, she took her sweet time in getting up and going to the kitchen. While she was gone I cased the room. Lots of books, paintings, and bones for Cuddles. I could have sworn that one of the bones was a dead ringer for a man's forearm.

It didn't take long for Miss Snerd to return with a fancy silver serving cart laden with brownies, coffee, and cream and sugar, as well as china plates and cups. This lady sure has class, I said to myself.

I told her what swell brownies she made. She told me to help myself. I told her that four were as many as I could pack in. We made some idle talk. I said that I admired all the books she had and asked if she liked Proust. She told me that he was a bit too French for her taste, and that she preferred James Joyce, Thomas Mann, and the poems of Edgar Guest. I could see that Miss Snerd was no dummy. Then she asked me to tell her about myself. For some reason, I felt that I could speak frankly and divulge some pretty personal stuff. I took a deep breath and informed her that I was five-eleven, weighed 180 pounds, except when I had had too many sweets and too many peanuts. I had brown hair and brown eyes, like quite a few other people, but what really set me off from the crowd was a birthmark that resembled a mango and surrounded my right armpit. I told her that I'd show it to her when we got to know each other better.

"I think we'd better get down to business, Mr. DeWitt." She yawned. "I'm usually in bed by this time."

Never keep a lady waiting, they say, so I got down to brass tacks, or whatever they're making tacks of these days. I told Miss Snerd pretty much all I knew about the missing girl, which wasn't worth more than a hill of beans, though come to think of it, with the price of beans these days . . . . Then I asked her for anything she knew that could help me locate her missing friend.

Turns out that she wasn't much help. Mona, she said, has a certain boyfriend, a baker Baker, who was very nice to her. I knew that already, and I knew about her passion for basketball. Ditto the chink food. I hadn't known, however, that she had an older brother who had worked a gig as a flagpole sitter until he ran off with a pharmacist from Kokomo, Indiana. The two were now living in Liechtenstein, which, I supposed, was somewhere out of state. She also informed me that she thought Mona had mentioned a man whose initials were "B.L." It was a long shot, since the only "B.L." that came to mind was "Black Llama." But I made a note to check on it as soon as I followed up on the lead about the brother and the pharmacist.

I didn't want to overstay my welcome, and so I shoveled a brownie into my mouth and another one into my shirt pocket. Apologizing to my hostess for having kept her from bed, I asked her to fetch my outerwear and I'd be on my way. She made quick time in retrieving my coat but informed me that Cuddles had polished off both my galoshes and hat. I could have sworn that I heard a loud belch from the other room.

I intended to walk home and breathe more of that bracing air that made early winter nights a delight. Outside, however, the snow was coming down in buckets and beginning to blanket the city. It was cold, bitterly so. There wasn't a bus in sight, and the only cab driver I saw gleefully made an obscene gesture when I tried flagging him down. I trudged along as best I could. I fell once and flattened the brownie that I thought was safely sequestered in my shirt pocket. "Egad," I cursed to myself.

At length I reached home, ready for a good night's sleep. I took my apartment key from my right shoe, where I always keep it, and prepared to unlock the door. There was no need: the door was open. I stood there transfixed. Within a minute or two I deduced that someone had been here and perhaps still was. I blamed myself for having left my .38 at the office but tiptoed in and yelled, "Come out, come out, whoever you are!" He did. Only from behind me. Then the lights went out.

12

It was daybreak when I awoke. The inside of my head throbbed like Gene Krupa was playing his drums; the outside sported a lump the size of the Himalayas. I managed to get to my feet and headed for the shower. The blast of water felt good. It would have felt better had I remembered to remove my clothes. But at least part of the stain from last night's brownie did come off my shirt. For every loss, there's a gain, for every dark cloud, there's . . . . Ah, never mind.

I downed a couple of aspirins. That helped to convince Krupa to take five. Meanwhile the Himalayas were diminishing to the scale of the Adirondacks. I toweled myself, put on my moth-eaten but nice-and-toasty robe, and surveyed the apartment to see what the lousy bastard who had busted in had swiped. Nothing! What could the thief have been looking for? It was a puzzle and a conundrum.

I fashioned a list of possible suspects. That got me nowhere. If it had been my ex, she would have flattened me with something heavier, say, a crowbar, which would have landed me in the infirmary or the city morgue. Mom was still pissed at me because I forgot to include a card with the secondhand can opener I had given her for Mother's Day. But I couldn't imagine that she would want to physically harm her sonny boy. No doubt there had been clients dissatisfied with services rendered. Yet break into my place and belt me on the noggin? True, Freddie Fuchsberger had threatened to fix me but good for having accidentally shot him when I was cleaning my gun. But it was only a flesh wound, and the doctors swore that he would recover and be able to have sex within six months or so. Besides, Freddie had died a year later from choking on a pig's knuckle in an uptown German *brauhaus*.

I had reached the end of my tether as far as suspects went when a 15-watt bulb flickered in my aching head. Could it have been the mystery man who kept threatening my client and me with calls and notes? It was a long shot, but I had gone through the short ones. What I really needed were sure shots, and only plenty of legwork, accompanied by luck and pluck, could deliver. I dressed quickly and skipped breakfast, figuring that the files in my office had some morsels hanging around.

The snow had stopped, but shovelers were busy cursing Mother Nature for her depravity. The language they were using was bluer than the Nile. I slipped and fell into a snowbank. Then I cursed Mother Nature too. Also Cuddles, who had deprived me of my galoshes. Traffic was snarled, and I didn't reach the office until late morning. I didn't find Dotty there, but my nose helped me to find the remains of a sardine sandwich that was nestling between a pair of women's panties and *War and Peace* in the bottom drawer of the file cabinet. I made a note to ask Dotty about the book.

But first things first: Liechtenstein and Mona's runaway brother. I called various acquaintances. No dice. Stuart the Stoolie thought Liechtenstein was an Atlantic City gambler who had had his legs broken after welshing on a bet; Morose Manny thought it was a small city in Pennsylvania that had a diner that served great buckwheat pancakes. Clyde Hickenlooper knew for sure that it was a kraut restaurant on West 46th but said to avoid it because the sauerkraut was too sour.

Having come up empty on the Liechtenstein business, I concentrated on who could have been the nogoodnik who had clobbered me. I started with the long shots and called Mom and the ex. Mom would be pleased as Punch to hear from me in any case. The ex wouldn't, but I'd uncurl the sneer on her lips when I told her that the alimony check's in the mail, or would be as soon as I found a stamp.

"Hello, Mom, this is sonny boy."

"What do you want?" Mom was always the caring type.

"I just thought I'd call and say 'hello.' By the way, did you go over to my place last evening?"

"What! Are you nuts? With all that snow I would go out? And even if I had, why would I go to see you? You know, sonny boy, you're a stupid moron. You're dumber than dog shit. You're . . . "

I could tell that Mom had fallen out on the wrong side of the bed. Too much gin. I tried to get on her good side. "Hey, Mom, aren't you even going to ask 'How are they hanging'?"

"Listen, you poor excuse for a son, I don't care if they've fallen off."

She hung up before I got the chance to ask if she was enjoying the can opener.

I fared better with my ex. She was out when I called.

Maybe it was the sardine sandwich that I had wolfed down, or maybe it was the drawing of a blazing cannon on the cover of *War and Peace*, but I was feeling the strong urge that men have felt since their days in the cave. So I went down the hall to the men's room and peed.

The good-looking dame who worked as secretary for Stanley Goniff, the lawyer, beamed me a big smile when I emerged from the men's room. I now had another strong urge. I might have mentioned that it had been some time since I had performed the horizontal rumba. It was time to practice a few steps again and do the dirty deed. In a word— no, make that three—I felt horny.

I made a list of all the eligible females I knew who might care to trip the light fantastic with me. It didn't take long. It was poor taste to try making it with Dotty, especially since the one time I had tried she dislocated my shoulder and bit me so hard that I needed a tetanus shot. I don't think that Dotty's a prude, and I certainly have had a few suspicions, having seen her bra and panties lying around the office at various times, particularly after she had asked if she could work late. Abigail Snerd was a real swell dish, but I'd be afraid that Cuddles would make a dish out of me if I tried to persuade his owner to take time out from James Joyce, Thomas Mann, and Edgar Guest to cavort with this here dick. The thought of coupling with Gardenia, aka Gonorrhea Gertie, spoke for itself and made the sardines swimming in my stomach swim for help.

What about Sadie Plotz? Sadie and I had enjoyed a few good rolls in the hay in our day, and we had also enjoyed having sex. I got the idea the last time we spoke that she wouldn't mind doing a little bit of this and that, whenever and wherever. The fact that it could also be with whomever wasn't bothering me at the moment.

I called Ma Bell's office where Sadie worked and asked to speak with her.

"*Como se llama?*" came a voice.

"I'd like to speak with Sadie Plotz, please. That's 'Plotz' as in 'hots'."

"*Como se llama?*" the voice repeated.

"Plotz! Plotz!" I yelled.

"*Sí señor. Como se llama?*"

I was getting nowhere fast with this Tijuana tamale. Frustrated—now in more ways than one—I hung up.

I was gnashing my teeth—or at least the ones that could be gnashed—when I made the connection. *Como se _llama_?* The Black _Llama_? I could have jumped for joy but settled for no longer gnashing my teeth. Could Ma Bell be harboring the notorious Black Llama? Was the Black Llama a spic? Was the Black Llama actually the tamale I had just spoken to?

My mind was awash in a whirlpool of wondering whys. (I tried saying that five times in a row but quit after the third try.) Now I was pretty certain that I was getting somewhere. My next step would be to contact Sadie Plotz and find out the score. But I wasn't about to arouse suspicion by calling her office back. I'd wait for her when she finished work.

They say things come in threes, and I was hoping for a couple more leads in the Mona case before seeing Sadie. No soap. I went out to a luncheonette around the block. I was famished and had some scrambled eggs, a bowl of chicken soup, and a chicken salad sandwich. I clucked a thank-you to the waitress and, being flush with the advance my client had given me, left a fifteen-cent tip. Betty at Ma's should only know.

No new clients lighted on my doorstep for the remainder of the afternoon. I was becoming concerned about Dotty and her whereabouts, but she called around 3:30 to say that she had overslept and wouldn't be able to get dressed and come in before closing time. I thought I heard a man's laugh in the background but concluded that we had a poor phone connection.

I left the office at 4:15 to make sure that I would be waiting for Sadie when she got off work. I took my .38 with me. The Black Llama also might be getting off work.

13

Sadie emerged from the elevator at 5:05. She was clutching the arm of a tall, swarthy man like it was a five-hundred-dollar bill.

"Hi, Sadie," I called. "Fancy meeting you here."

Sadie Plotz looked as though she was about to do so.

"Ah . . . oh, hi there, Mr. DeWitt." She gave me a wink and said that she hadn't seen me since we were celebrating my wife's birthday some years ago. That was a lie, of course. Sadie never met my wife. I suppose she didn't want Mr. Tall and Swarthy to think that I was an old beau.

"Aren't you going to introduce me to your friend?" I asked. Her scowl told me that she didn't want to, but I had her trapped.

"Why certainly. Dick DeWitt, I'd like you to meet Pancho Juan O'Brien. Juan, this is Dick DeWitt. He's the husband of one of my oldest and dearest friends." She was laying it on pretty thick, but I was more interested in her friend's unusual name.

"Glad to meet you, Mr. O'Brien," I said, glad-handing him. "By the way, were you born here?"

Tall and Swarthy pumped my hand vigorously and replied: "*Mucho gusto*." I think he was referring to the wind that had begun to swirl.

"No, I mean, were you born here in this country?"

He kept shaking my hand, smiling, and bubbling *"mucho gusto, mucho gusto."* He had nice white teeth, I noticed.

Sadie intervened. "Dick, Mr. O'Brien doesn't speak much English yet. He came here from Montenegro only a few months ago."

I wasn't convinced that the handsome mug wasn't a spic, but I let it drop. For now. I made a mental note to call Sadie when she was alone at home, which wouldn't be tonight if she could help it. She was dragging Tall, Swarthy, and Presumably Montenegrin down the block before I could say *"adios."*

A fair amount of snow remained on the sidewalks. I stopped at a nearby Army and Navy Surplus store, forked over some simoleons for a used pair of galoshes, and trudged home. Halfway there, I remembered to put them on.

Before I could open the door to my apartment, nosey old Mrs. Heidegger lurched from her doorway to inquire if I had heard the news. "What news?" I asked. She said, "Any news." I needed a drink.

Three fingers of Jack Daniel's and I was ready to call the ex to say that I would mail the check first thing in the morning. This time when I called she was at home. Unfortunately. I thought that she'd be grateful that the monthly alimony was soon to take wings and fly her way. Instead she snarled that it was about time. She further suggested that I do something to myself that struck me as being anatomically impossible and more than a little perverted. I freshened my drink.

I wasn't very hungry for my evening meal but fixed a peanut butter and jelly sandwich, topped with catsup and a pickle, and skipped the cupcakes. It was 7:30. Too early to sleep. I figured I'd wander off to the Elbow. What the hell. Sitting around trying to solve Mona's disappearance wasn't giving me any jollies.

Why the joint was packed, I couldn't figure, but the gang was all there. I spotted Shorty Tallwood with a couple of his pals plotting something or other that most likely would cause him to return to the pen. Billy Two Shoes was coming on to a couple of peroxide blonde barflies in the corner. His tie resting in his stein of beer, Rudy Tooty Vanderhander was asleep at another table, snoring. And of course no gathering would have been complete without Gardenia Gertie, who had planted herself on some man's lap and was vigorously resisting his efforts to remove her. They were all there. My kind of people.

I ambled to the bar and told Gus that I wanted to take care of my tab. He said that he didn't know I had a cat. "I want to take care of my tab, Gus, not my tabby." I felt sorry for my favorite bartender. A rumor had it that he had lost some hearing during the war. Another one said that he had only told the military draft board that he couldn't hear in his right ear and the board declared him unfit to serve. Gus didn't ask me to repeat myself. He reckoned the bill. I paid it and started a new one by ordering a Cuba Libre.

"Hey, DeWitt," Gus said, "I got so excited when you picked up your tab that I forgot to give you this note that Light Fingers Louie left for you. He said he tried to get you on the phone earlier but that your line was busy."

I read the note. Louie had come up with another lead. I hoped that it was better than the first one, but I was skeptical. "Mr. DeWitt," it ran, "go to the Sisters of Pleurisy Convent School on West 17th St. and ask to speak with Sister Semper Fidelis. I hear she might know something about Mona. By the way, the other sisters call her 'Sister Semper Fi,' but I'd be careful. I hear she's a handful."

Sure, Louie, and I'm best friends with the pope. But it was a lead that I decided to follow the next day. For now I'd enjoy my Cuba Libre, have a second one, and tell Gertie that I liked the tattered slip she was wearing.

I went home and read a little before calling it a night. First I skimmed a few pages about a pansy orchid grower named Nero Wolfe. Couldn't stand it. Who'd ever take a gumshoe like that seriously? The same went for another gumshoe with the silly name of Sam Spade. Why did their authors ever create losers like them, I wondered. What crap!

I fell asleep almost as soon as my head touched the pillow but tossed and turned the whole night. I can recall at least one bad dream I had where I ripped the mask off the Black Llama and found that it was Sister Semper Fidelis, who started running away. I gave chase but tripped over Gardenia Gertie, who was playing dominoes with Light Fingers Louie on the sidewalk. I reached in my back pocket for my gat but pulled out a sardine sandwich instead. I started yelling as loud as I could. A loud pounding on the wall accompanied by cursing from the neighbor next door woke me. I seem to recall telling him "and you too!" I reached under the covers for my alarm clock. It was only 4:15. I tried to fall asleep again but couldn't. I must have counted a thousand sheep. No sheep next time, I promised myself.

Frazzled but determinated to pursue Louie's latest lead, I headed downtown. The Sisters of Pleurisy Convent School had seen better days, though, of course, hadn't we all? Wedged between a pawnbroker's shop and a store with a sign that advised "We sell and lease cockatoos," the school had outer walls encrusted with grime and several windows that lacked panes. Clearly the school had taken a vow of poverty. As for vows of chastity and obedience I couldn't say.

I banged the door knocker and noticed a graffito that warned: "Abandon all hope, ye who enter here." I recalled hearing that expression before. I think my ex had written it on a piece of paper and then taped it to our bedroom door. Say that for her, the ex always did have a sense of humor.

The door opened slowly and a stoop-shouldered elderly man eyed me and asked what I wanted. He was the gardener, it turned out. There wasn't any garden, but the sisters, he explained, always prayed for one and were keeping him on hand just in case. I told him that I wanted to see Sister Semper Fidelis. He scratched his head and looked puzzled. "You want to become a nun?" I assured him that I would rather take all my meals at Ma's and go home each night with Betty. I guess he was convinced. "Follow me, young man, Sister Semper Fidelis is in the pool room."

The "pool room" turned out to be a small office with a desk and a few chairs. The room had got its name, I guessed, from the pools of water that had dripped from the cracked ceiling and formed on the bare floor. Obviously the good sisters had omitted St. Philoctetes, the patron saint of plasterers, from their prayers.

Sister Semper Fidelis was sitting behind the desk doing a crossword puzzle and munching on a stalk of celery. She was elderly—in her late 80s, I'd say—but otherwise seemed fit. She looked up when I entered and adjusted her wimple, which had fallen down when she looked up. She eyed me suspiciously through the pair of binoculars that hung around her neck.

"Well, what is?" she barked. "I haven't finished doing the words across let alone the ones down. Do you think I have all day to waste, you damn fool?"

I attributed this mild display of temper to the difficulty she was having with her wimple. I introduced myself and said that I had reason to believe that she might know something about a six-five blonde who carried around a basketball.

She frowned. "Who wants to know?"

"Well, I do," I explained.

She took another gander at me through her binoculars and adjusted her wimple. "Tell me," she asked, "what religion are you?"

I told her that Dad had been an atheist but Mom was a devout agnostic and had demanded from Dad that I be raised a Quaker. I had gone to a Quaker school for several years until I began to feel my oats and slugged the headmaster. I had been thrown out for that and so was he for having slugged me back. Since then I had searched for faith and the meaning of life but so far without success.

"Well, at least you're not one of those nasty Protestants the Devil sent," she fumed.

Sister Semper Fidelis took another chomp of celery and then went back to her puzzle. She looked up a few minutes later and seemed surprised to see me. "What do you want? I've seen your face before, haven't I?"

I reminded myself to kick Louie in the nuts the next time he sent me on a wild goose chase. I was also about to tell Sister to go take a flying leap, but good manners and the knowledge that I was in a sanctified place stopped me. I got up from my chair and stuck my tongue out at her. She couldn't see this because the wimple had once again fallen down.

Suddenly she sat upright and adjusted the wimple. "Wait a minute, you poor excuse for a Quaker. Did you say you were looking for a six-five blonde with a basketball? Why of course I know her!" She told me to sit down again and stick my tongue back in my mouth.

"That's Mona Tuvachevsky-Smith you're talking about. I just call her 'stilts.' She used to be a student at the school. She palled around with a girl named Gertie something-or-other, whom the other girls unanimously voted 'most likely to become a tramp.' Had to let Gertie go when she was found shacking up with the pawnbroker next door. Wonder what's become of the trollop?"

I was not about to say but made a note to ask Gertie about Mona the next time I was frequenting the Elbow.

"Sister, about Mona . . . "

"Who? Oh, yes, Mona. Mona showed up a few weeks ago. I thought she had come back to return the silverware that went missing at the time she took a leave of absence, but she said she'd returned to seek sanctuary. She needed to hide out for a while. Well, we don't let just anyone take sanctuary here, especially if they've stolen our silverware, but we're a forgiving bunch of sisters. We also were in bad need of someone to play center for our basketball team in the Nuns Net League. Our previous center, a sweet young thing by the name of Clorinda Katootch, surprised us all by leaving the school a couple of months after some accident or other at the pawnbroker's. She was getting too fat around the middle to play a good center in any case."

Sister Semper Fidelis returned to her puzzle and celery, but I drew her back by asking if Mona were here and if I could speak to her.

"Why of course you can speak to her, young man. I noticed that you had a tongue. She's not here now. She's on the road for a few days with the rest of the team. But they'll be back the day after tomorrow ... or is it the day after that?"

I gave her my card. She thanked me and said that she didn't receive many cards these days, except at Halloween. I asked her to have Mona call as soon as she returned. "From where?" the good sister asked.

It was still a longshot.

14

I had a quick lunch after my visit to the Sisters of Pleurisy and then went to the office. I told Joe the elevator man that the slimeball landlord still hadn't fixed the sign on my door and that I was fed up. He asked if lunch had been good as well as filling. I took the stairs and ran into the same tramp who had been darkening our stairwell a couple of days ago. I kicked him, but not hard and not for long.

And speaking of tramps, I was glad to see that Dotty was back at work. She looked tired as hell but had a smile on her face the size of both of Primo Carnera's fists. We shot the breeze for a while. Then Dotty went back to Proust—volume three, she said—and I thumbed through my proverbial little black book. I didn't find any proverbs, and I had last seen any of the skirts listed about the time Julius Caesar had crossed some river to fight his enemy Pompous. Horny, horny, horny. I couldn't get doing you-know-what off my mind. Watching Proust's number-one fan playing with her hair wasn't helping matters.

The next forty-eight hours dragged by like a turtle on sleeping pills. No new ideas for finding Mona, no new clients. I moped around the office during the day, puttered around the apartment at night. Paid the landlord, sent the ex her alimony check. This is what you call a life?

Then things picked up. I was seated at my desk reading the latest issue of *The Police Gazette* and telling Dotty, who was trimming my hair, to go easy. I liked the cheap—actually, free—haircuts she gave me every month or so, but she had a bad habit of sticking me with the scissors. Once she nearly took off my right earlobe. Now as the phone rang she jumped and so did the scissors, which all but took off the left one.

"Dick DeWitt, Privates Investigator." Try as I might, I could never convince Dotty that she need not mimic the sign on our office door. "Yes, he's terribly busy"—but I could and did convince her to lie—"but I'll see if he can come to the phone."

On this occasion I actually was terribly busy. The blood from my left earlobe was spewing out and down my white Arrow shirt. "Who is it?" I mouthed silently to Dotty. She wrote on the pad that was on my desk and not yet completely covered with my blood: "Sister Semper Fidelis."

I yanked the phone out of her hand. "Yes, Sister, do you have news for me, I hope ... What do you mean, 'what news?' ... No, Sister, I didn't call you, you called me ... Yes, that's right ... Sister, you called me just now!" By this time I wanted to grab her by the throat, pull down her wimple, and announce that I had become a Protestant. But I kept my temper and finally did ascertain that Mona had returned and would call me as soon as possible. I thanked the good Sister, who in turn asked me to say "hello" to that nice Mr. DeWitt.

A big smile attached itself to my puss. "Dotty, we're in business. This last lead is panning out. Our case is fast heading for a close."

"That's just great, Mr. D," she said, gently wiping the blood off my ear with my tie. "Should you call Mr. Baker with the news?"

Dotty had a point. She had two of them actually, but that's another story. "No, I think it best to wait until I tie up the whole kit and kaboodle and surprise him with it."

I was so pleased with the way things were breaking that I invited Dotty for lunch. Dutch treat naturally. We locked up the office and walked downstairs. We got a lot of bug-eyed stares while walking over to Ye Olde Foods Emporium, a chow joint that I heard was decent as long as you didn't go there with high hopes. I couldn't decide if the stares were for Dotty, who had more curves than Carl Hubbell, or for me, holding my tie to my left earlobe. The grub was odd at the Emporium. Dotty ordered the fish and chips, which tasted more like spagetti and meatballs. I had the canard à l'orange, or so the menu claimed. Frankly, I thought the canard was a canard.

We returned to the office and waited for Mona to call. We waited, and when we had finished, we waited some more. Nothing. Nada. Niente. Zilch mixed with bupkus. From time to time Dotty startled me with a shriek of laughter. She said Proust was really funny, although not nearly as humorous as Kafka. Around half-past four I told Dotty to take her Proust, shelve it, and go home.

I was trying on—just for fun of course—the pair of Dotty's underwear that she had left in the file cabinet, when the phone rang. I was annoyed at the interruption.

"Dick DeWitt here. What can I do for you?"

"Mr. DeWitt, this is Mona."

My heart skipped a beat. Dotty's panties were much too tight. Trying to control my voice, which had become a high soprano, I said, "Mona, I've been looking all over this great, crazy town for you. Where are you?" She gave me an address on the city's east side and told me to meet her there at 7:30 sharp. "Come alone," she demanded, "and whatever you do, don't tell dear Mr. Baker until after we've met." I could hear a basketball bouncing in the background. I suppose I could have been suspicious but not of a convent school girl with a gentleman for a boyfriend. Nonetheless, I oiled and cleaned my .38 before leaving the office.

I had plenty of time before meeting Mona. The air was crisp, but there was no sign of the white excrement falling from the heavens. I walked to the east side of town and stopped for dinner at a Mexican cantina, where I ordered huevos rancheros. The waiter brought me duck.

Mona's place was on the ground floor of a small apartment building. I pushed the buzzer. She buzzed me in. I was not surprised to see how tall she was, but I was surprised to find her wearing a thick fur coat. I figured she was cold, although five seconds into this hothouse and I was sweating like a pig.

"Aren't you warm wearing that coat?" I asked.

"No," she said. I waited for her next sentence but there wasn't one.

"Were you about to go some place?" A good private eye knows how to ask questions that get right to the point.

I didn't have to wait long for a response. Only it didn't come from Mona. "*Sí, sí, señor.*" I wheeled around. It was Sadie's amigo, the Black Llama, and he was pointing a nasty-looking revolver at me.

"Let's discuss this," I said, to which he sneered. I was getting nowhere fast and he, for all I knew, had an itchy trigger finger.

Now I was sweating even more and it wasn't only because of the heater in the hand of Señor Black Llama or the temperature in the apartment. I had surreptitiously and secretly felt for my rod in my back pocket, only to discover that I had forgotten to bring it.

"Mona, what's up? Who is this man and why is he holding a gun?"

"It's a long story, Mr. DeWitt, but I guess you deserve an explanation. His name is Miguel Malvado, and he used to teach me advanced calculus at the convent school. I never learned much, however. I was never good at math, and he spoke little English. By the way, Señor Malvado was a priest in his country before he got defrocked for staging a cockfight and bribing one of the cocks to take a fall."

"But what's he got to do with your disappearance? Don't you know or care that Mr. Baker is frantic with worry about you?" I saw a tear come to her eye but decided that she was only allergic to her fur coat.

She smiled. "Don't you get it, Mr. DeWitt? Mr. Baker is a helluva nice guy, but he's also the most boring schlub I've ever met. Has halitosis, too. I need the bread since there's no place for a lady to play professional basketball. And playing basketball is what I do best, aside from crocheting." She paused to give an endearing pat to her basketball, which was resting on a nearby chair. "So Señor Malvado and I decided to take away some of the baker's bread, if you know what I mean. We were stringing out our sting, figuring that the longer we waited, the more lover boy would be willing to pay once he received a ransom note. But you had to get involved and get too close to discovering what was happening." She smiled. "You're what's known as a goddamned pain in the ass, a term I learned from the Sisters of Pleurisy. And now," she nodded to her confederate, "I'm afraid we'll have to silence Mr. DeWitt forever."

I didn't want to be silenced forever. I didn't even want to be silenced for now. My life raced before me, the good times and bad, the pleasures and regrets, Dotty's panties, and my mom's can opener.

Mona motioned for her partner in crime to let me have it. Malvado cocked his gun. "*Adiós, amig...,*" he started to say, when a fury straight out of hell burst through the door.

"You don't walk out on me after doing it only four times!" The shrill voice belonged to Sadie Plotz, who began to struggle with the gaucho wannabe for his gun. Meanwhile I tackled Mona, who went down with a thud and hit her head hard on a suitcase. I found some yarn that she was crocheting with and bound her hands and feet. I tried to stuff the basketball into her mouth but it was too big. The basketball, that is. Then I turned to help Sadie, who didn't need my assistance. She was firing at Malvado and chasing him out the front door before she tripped on the doormat. She might have winged him, but I couldn't tell.

I went over to straighten the doormat. Then I helped Sadie up. "You did good, Sadie Plotz," I told her.

I called the police and explained that we had an emergency situation on our hands. They arrived an hour and forty-five minutes later and took Mona into custody. Sadie suggested that we go back to her place for a quickie, but I declined the offer. Another time, I told her. She seemed miffed and grumbled something about a lack of gratitude for having saved my life. But I needed some fresh air and time to sort through all that had been happening since Mr. Baker had first come to see me. I said good night to Sadie as we walked out of the building and headed for our respective apartments. It had started to snow again. I raised the collar on my coat and thought of the galoshes I wished I had brought.

15

Exhaustion hit me with a series of one-two punches by the time I reached home. My body felt like a football the Chicago Bears had used to scrimmage with all season. I owed some of my fatigue to the duck I ate. Eating duck for both lunch and dinner was no easy matter. Nor was the episode with Mona and the Black Llama. But the case was all but closed now. Finito. I sank into bed without setting the alarm clock. Tomorrow would come soon enough.

And it did. My brain was racing a hundred miles an hour by the time the city was waking, yawning, and getting ready for what lay ahead. I wondered about Mona and what craziness had made an ordinary six-foot-five blonde who loved to dribble a basketball turn to crime. And I reflected upon my near-miss with Mr. Death. If Sadie Plotz had not arrived in the nick of time, I would be dead meat on a cold slab in a cold morgue in a cold city on a cold November morning. The thought made my blood run cold.

The heat in the apartment came on, and I felt less cold. I got up, splashed water on my face, and fixed some Quaker Oats and piping hot coffee. I wondered what the temperature was outside.

All this rumination, I knew, was an excuse not to do what I had to do. It was still early, but I called my client to tell him about last evening. He was heartbroken, as I knew he'd be. No pastryman wants to be taken for a patsy. And this pastryman, with all his dough, would need a lot of time and care to heal his wounds and make his yeast rise again. My heart went out to the poor schmuck. I told him that if there was anything I could do to help, he should let me know. I also told him that I would send him a bill for the remainder of my fees and expenses, payable upon receipt. Hell, I had earned every penny of it.

Little snow had accumulated overnight. I walked to the office in a good mood and bounded up the eight flights of stairs. It didn't last. The mood, not the stairs. The scumbag landlord had repainted the sign on my office to read: "Dicks DeWitt: Private Investigator." I unlocked the door and found that someone, probably Joe the elevator man, had slipped a note under it. It contained a single word, "*Muerte*," and was signed "The Black Llama." I knew that my adversary would show up sooner or later, and probably sooner. And his accomplices? The one or ones who had delivered threats in English on the phone and in writing? The tamale at Sadie's office? People I had interviewed? I took my .38 from the file cabinet and placed it on the desk. Being a gumshoe had its days. Trouble was, one never knew what any particular day would bring.

16

I didn't have to wait long. A loud banging on the door followed by "Open up, you creep" got my full attention.

I grabbed my .38 and said, "Come on in, you lousy spic bastard. I'm ready for you."

"And we're ready for you, too, you pimple on society's ass."

The door flew open and there stood two of the city's finest: Detectives John "Jack the Ripper" O'Meara and Tony "Holy Canoli" Bruttafaccia from the 13th Precinct. From where I was sitting, their revolvers looked like cannons and were aimed squarely at me.

"Drop it, dickhead," O'Meara ordered, "or we'll turn your ugly puss into Swiss cheese."

I dropped my rod faster than I had dropped my old high school flame when I learned that she had the crabs.

"Okay, boys, take it easy. What's this all about? So I promised to buy a ticket to the Policemen's Ball and broke my promise. You come all the way here just to collect?"

"Shuddup, wiseass," snarled O'Meara. "We got a tip that you did in some chink waiter last week. You didn't pay for your food, but you're going to pay for this, DeWitt. Cuff him, Tony."

"Hey, you can't do this to me," I protested, as Bruttafaccia stood me up, put my hands behind my back, and threw on the shackles. "I didn't do nothing. You can't do this to me. I got my rights!"

"Oh yeah? Let's see what the Lieutenant has to say about that. Let's get this bag of horse manure out of here, Tony."

We took the short walk from my office to the elevator and waited for Joe the elevator man to bring it up. The door opened and out stepped my secretary Dotty. "Good morning, Mr. DeWitt. Sorry that I'm a little late but I was reading *Moby Dick* while I was having my cereal and I just couldn't put it down." She giggled, as only Dotty could. "The book, not the corn flakes."

She started to walk away but then turned. "Say, who are these men, Mr. D? Are you going out for coffee with them? Just in case someone should call, when shall I say you'll be back?"

O'Meara, who along with his partner had been standing with their mouths open at the sight of my shapely Gal Friday, snickered, "When it's a cold day in hell."

Dotty looked puzzled and seemed about to ask if hell had cold days when I cut her short.

"Just call my lawyer, Dotty, and have him come down to the 13th Precinct. And pronto."

"But you don't have a lawyer, Mr. D. The last one you had, that nice Mr. Finagler, said that he wouldn't help you if you were drowning because you stiffed him his fees."

"Then forget Finagler," I yelled over my shoulder as the suits were pushing me into the elevator. "Call my mother, call my ex-wife, call the mayor, call anyone!"

Once we were all inside, Joe, whose eyes were opened wider than the wide Missouri, asked which floor we wanted.

"The penthouse is for us, don't you think, Tony?" O'Meara chuckled.

"I'm sorry, gents, but there's no penthouse in this building, although the view from the top floor isn't bad." Either Joe was on the sauce again or was more stupid than I had imagined.

"Listen, pinhead," O'Meara snarled, "get us down to the ground right now or you'll be spending the night in the slammer." And following those gentle words he slapped Joe on the back of the head.

Outside, Bruttafaccia shoved me into the backseat of the patrol car. In under five minutes we reached the 13th Precinct, a forlorn gray building that had witnessed buckets of tears, countless bruises, and untold broken hearts. I feared that I was about to add to that sad collection, and for no good reason whatsoever.

We walked upstairs to the second-story office of Lieutenant Andrew "Andy the Assburn" Ashburn, a grizzled old-school copper who took no guff but gave plenty. He was sitting behind a cluttered desk and in front of a wall graced by photos of the mayor, J. Edgar Hoover, and Babe Ruth.

"Well, well, well. If it isn't Dirty Dick DeWitt himself. Fancy meeting the lousy shithead private eye."

I could tell that the Assburn was no more pleased to see me than I was to see him. I was not slow to pick up subtleties.

"Listen, Lieutenant, I didn't kill any chink waiter. What am I doing here?"

"You're doing here, DeWitt, because word has it that you did in the Chinaman and sent him off to his Happy Hunting Grounds or wherever the slant-eyes go when they kick the bucket."

"Says who?"

"I don't have to tell you but I will since I'm a nice guy." He looked behind me. "And wipe those smirks off your mugs, O'Meara and Bruttafaccia, or you'll both be back walking beats on the other side of the river!" He looked at me again. "Now, as I was about to say before the mick and the goombah so rudely interrupted, word came from an anonymous caller who seemed to know quite a lot about the event and your part in it."

"Did the caller have an accent?"

"As a matter of fact he did. Sounded like a spic to me. Why do you ask?"

"Because I'm on a case where some Latin sweetheart has already kidnapped a dame, threatened me, and was probably the one who killed the waiter. I bet that the bastard has tried to set me up to take the rap for the murder."

The Assburn lit a cigar, blew a few rings, and grinned. "You never know, DeWitt, but (puff, puff) you're our prime suspect, at least until another one comes along."

"You've got no evidence against me, Lieutenant. You don't even know that I was ever at the slop joint."

"Wanna bet? We've got your prints on the chopsticks and some dishes." He blew another ring. "Now what do you say to that, smart boy?"

I was astonished. I asked him when he got my prints. He said the forensics man got them yesterday.

"Yesterday!"

"Yeah, yesterday. You don't think these Chinamen throw out their chopsticks or wash their dishes every day, do you?"

I was flabbergasted. I explained what had happened and asked what killed the old guy.

"We think someone, probably you, slipped some arsenic into his moo goo gai pan, but we won't know for sure until the lab report comes back in a couple of days." He smiled. "Want to confess before then and save the taxpayers of this fair city a few bucks, shamus?"

I was sweating like a greased pig. The Black Llama had put me in a tough spot, all right, and I didn't know how I was going to squeeze out of it. "I want to call a lawyer, Lieutenant."

"Sure, sure. We'll let you do that. Did you think we were going to get the rubber hose and beat the crap out of you until you cried 'uncle' and confessed? We're not those kinds of policemen, are we boys?"

"Nah," said Bruttafaccia with a sly grin on his swarthy face. Jack the Ripper O'Meara looked tight-lipped and remained ominously silent.

"Come on, boys," the Assburn said, "let DeWitt call his shyster and see if he can wiggle out of this one."

The trio left the room and the telephone to me. I called the office. "Hello, Dotty, were you able to get me some help yet?"

"Not really, but I did finish a couple more chapters of *Moby Dick*. That's really a great book, even if it's only about a whale. You should read it sometime."

And you should go, I thought, and . . . . Never mind. I'm in too much of a jam to deal with this ditzy airhead. "Did you call anyone, Dotty?"

"Oh sure, Mr. D, I called your mom and your ex-wife."

"And?"

"Well, your mom said something about a can opener you had given her and, funny, she also said something about hell freezing over. She sounded just like those men you went for coffee with."

Good old Mom. "What about my ex-wife?"

"When she heard that a couple of men had handcuffed you and were taking you for coffee, she started laughing hysterically. She said she hadn't laughed as hard since the last Laurel and Hardy comedy, and that she hoped they give you a lot of free coffee to drink. That was nice of her, don't you think? I don't know why you always say she's such a nasty person, Mr. D."

"I guess I just misjudged her, Dotty," I said through gritted teeth. "Now keep trying to get me a lawyer or I'll fillet your *Moby Dick*."

I hung up and waited for the Assburn and his goons to return. I didn't have to wait long since they apparently were standing outside the door listening to my call.

"No lawyer yet, DeWitt? Gee, and here I thought you were a friend of the bar. Or is it 'bars'?"

That one got a horse laugh from O'Meara and Bruttafaccia, who both knew which side of the toast to butter for favors and promotions.

"Tell you what, DeWitt, we're going to let you go for now, although we expect you to be visiting again real soon. Christmas is just around the corner, so you better get your shopping done before you come back here for the holidays."

The Assburn took a few more puffs on his stogie, which now was threatening to burn his fingers. "But you'll like it here with us, won't he boys? We'll have some real yuletide cheer and maybe find a red suit for you to wear." Puff, puff. "With stripes, of course."

Tweedle Dum and Tweedle Dee laughed again.

"And maybe Bruttafaccia can dress up as Santa Claus and come down the Precinct chimney." The Lieutenant looked at Holy Canoli. "Of course he's as fat as Fatty Arbuckle. He'd probably get stuck."

This time only O'Meara laughed.

"Okay, beat it, gumshoe, and go have a good time spying through keyholes on cheating husbands and wives. But don't make no plans to go south and pick up a tan. Matter of fact, don't make plans to leave the city, period." Puff, puff. "And," he said, pointing his cigar at me, "I promise you'll enjoy Christmas here with us."

"That's real white of you, Lieutenant," I said about five seconds before either O'Meara or Bruttafaccia slapped me on the back of the head. I was about to ask my pleasant company if they knew what dirty nickels were made of, but I wasn't in the mood for more physical abuse.

I walked out of the office, down the stairs, and out of the building. The cold sleet outside felt better than the hell inside.

17

The sleet came down harder as I walked back to my office, but I didn't mind. It was lunchtime, but I wasn't hungry. I was in big trouble with the police. And let's not forget the Black Llama. Funny how problems can make you forget about food and sleet and such things.

I didn't feel like answering any nosey questions that Joe the elevator man was bound to ask, so I climbed the eight flights of stairs to the office, which I often did in any case. I looked at the sign on my office door, "Dicks DeWitt: Private Investigator," and wondered how long it would be up there before I lost my job or my life and the scumbag landlord found a new tenant.

"Mr. D, you're back so soon!"

Nothing like an understanding secretary to cheer one up. "Yeah, I was getting tired of the java, and besides, it wasn't my brand."

"What brand do you like, Mr. D? Maxwell House? Chase and Sanborn? Eight O'Clock? If you let me know I'll be sure to keep some here in the office."

"Why don't you go for lunch, Dotty?"

"I was just thinking the same thing, Mr. D. Can I bring you back anything?"

"No, Dotty, but take your time. I'll handle things here."

Once Little Miss Genius took her sweet fanny out I settled back in my swivel chair to swivel a few thoughts as to how I was going to get out of the worst mess of my life. Well, second-worst mess. I had momentarily forgotten that I used to be married to Frankenstein's daughter.

As I saw matters, I had to pursue the Black Llama and keep the Assburn and his gorillas off my back at the same time. And the longer it took for me to catch the former and clip his wool, the shorter would be my freedom from the graft-dirtied clutches of the latter. Good luck, I told myself, and made a note to start my Christmas shopping and card writing a lot earlier than usual.

I needed help. That's for sure. Was there anyone I knew who could help me catch the greaser? Was there anyone who could convince the local gendarmes that I wasn't their man?

Presto, the light went on. I hadn't thought of retired police sergeant Philip "Polish Phil" Mazurki since I munched a few pierogies with him more than a year ago. George Washington, I had learned, was first in war, first in peace, and first in the hearts of his countrymen. Polish Phil, as I recall, was first on the take, first on the make, and first in the donut shop. The fact was that downing too many of those filled or fried sinkers did in his gall bladder and forced him to take early retirement on a small pension, handsomely supplemented by the years of graft he had accumulated. Phil had given new meaning to the word "corruption" and had become a legend for many cops and an icon for almost as many. He still must be pretty well off, I reckoned, if he hasn't spent it all on dames by this time. The odd thing was that once a dame with any looks whatsoever saw him in the daylight she took off as fast as she could, leaving his pot belly, bad teeth, and slightly crossed eyes to ogle the next broad who caught his eye, although I was never certain which eye it was.

But Phil was a good sort as far as I was concerned. He went after those he was inclined to go after with the tenacity of a bulldog, could be honest if the need really arose, and was loyal to those he called his friends. Due to a small favor

I did for him, I had become one of those friends and was now wondering if he could help me in return. It was worth a try. I strode over to Dotty's desk and fingered through the directory until I found "Mazurki, Philip." I dialed the number.

"The Mazurki residence," announced a voice in the throes of laryngitis or an awful cold.

"Hi. Is Phil there?"

"No, I'm afraid that Mr. Mazurki is out attending to his affairs."

You've got that right, I thought, wondering who the hoity-toity guy giving me the info was. "Do you know when he'll be back?"

"Mr. Mazurki is a man of indeterminate hours," he explained. "But I'll certainly inform him of your call. Kindly give me your name and number, if you please."

Either this mug was a male version of Emily Post or knew that lady's book of etiquette by heart. What the hell was he doing with a slob like the Polack, I wondered. Had Phil hired a butler? Anyway, I gave him my name and both my office and home numbers and asked him to have Phil get back to me as soon as possible.

No sooner did I hang up than Dotty returned. She was out of breath. "I just had the most wonderful sandwich for lunch," she announced.

I knew that I shouldn't have asked, but I did.

"It was a tuna on rye at that new place that opened last week next to Woolworth's. I'm going back for more tomorrow and maybe the day after that, too.

"Dotty, I thought you disliked tuna."

"Oh I do, Mr. D, but it seems only right that I eat it while I'm reading *Moby Dick*."

And it seemed only right at that point that I should get out of the office. I took the stairs once again to avoid Joe and walked to a nearby deli, where I wolfed down two hot dogs smothered with sauerkraut, mustard, and plenty of diced onions, and washed them down with a celery tonic. I was in the mood for a stroll to help clear my fogged mind, but it was still sleeting. Besides, I was hoping that Phil had called or soon would.

Joe was standing by the elevator when I returned and gave me a big greeting. I had no choice but to ride up with him and hope that the alcohol on his breath would not knock me out. "Geez, Mr. DeWitt, those were two tough-looking pals you were with. Your secretary Dotty told me that they were taking you for coffee. Was it good?"

I felt like a ping-pong ball battered back and forth between first one clunkhead and then another. The second one was reading when I entered my office. She managed to look both disturbed and pleasantly excited at the same time. "Did you know, Mr. D, that a whale has tons of sperm?"

I confessed to her that I hadn't given much thought to the matter nor would in all likelihood lose sleep over it either. I asked if anyone had called. She said no, but given her spellbound concentration on the big fish's sperm count there was room for doubt.

No calls by four o'clock, and so I sent Dotty and the big sperm boy home. Having nothing waiting for me at my own home except some stale leftovers, the radio, and a couple of magazines, I decided to stay for a while. I played with my gun (no, not that one) and leafed through a couple of old cases that I had failed to settle to my satisfaction or, even more, to the clients' satisfaction. Can't win them all, I thought, not in this kind of tough, dog-eat-dog world we live in. I grunted, put on my coat and hat, and was halfway out the door just a few minutes before five when the phone rang.

"Hello? Hello? That you, Phil?"

"No, *señor*. It's your *amigo*. You know, the one who's going to get you. *Hasta luego, gringo*." And with that the sonofabitch hung up.

It was one of those days.

18

And it wasn't over yet. After this most recent threatening call from the Llama, I decided to carry my .38 with me at all times. Never could tell when he might try to take me out, and it seemed pretty certain that he was going to try. Armed, I locked the office door and exited the building. The sleet had lightened to a fine drizzle, which was pricking at the umbrellas of workers on their way home after another boring day on the job. My day had at least not been boring, although I gladly would have traded my tryst with the Assburn and his baboons and the call from El Greaser for a nice extended yawn. Meanwhile I wondered if the Llama was somewhere among the passersby just waiting to slip a little lead or a shiv into me. As I walked I kept my hand on my piece, which I was carrying in my coat pocket. At one point I almost pulled it out when some dame, who was yakking with another one and paying no attention to traffic, nearly poked my eye out with her umbrella. She excused herself, and I settled for giving her a good shove that sent her into the arms of the other yakker.

I decided to stop at Ma's for supper. I was hoping that Betty's tour of duty had finished, but my favorite waitress was there to greet me when I arrived.

"Well, well, if it isn't Boston Blackie himself. I thought by this time J. Edgar Hoover would have called you to help clean up the nation's crime. What's the matter? You got an unlisted number?"

"It's unlisted for you, Betty, although I doubt if you could figure out how to use a phone even if you had someone dialing for you."

Betty didn't like that one bit. "Okay, DeWitt, let's cut out the nice talk. Know what you want or do you want to see a menu? Sorry, but the menu ain't like the comics. It only has words, but I'll explain them to you."

The day had depressed my spirits, and I wasn't in the mood to continue this palaver. I ordered the meatloaf platter, which came with mashed potatoes and succotash. I picked at the food half-heartedly but still managed to down it and a slab of pumpkin pie and a cup of coffee afterwards. I left Betty a nickel tip, realizing that it would be the last tip I would give her if the Llama had anything to say about it.

The drizzle had stopped when I left Ma's. It didn't take me long to get back to my apartment, where I threw off my clothes, took a hot shower, and poured myself a good helping of sneaky pete. I turned on the radio but wasn't in the mood for the crime story it was featuring. I picked up a magazine but couldn't concentrate on any of the articles. Then the phone rang, giving me hope that Polish Phil was the caller. He wasn't.

"Well, sonny boy, I see that you're not in the cooler. What did you do this time? Why did they let you out?"

Good old Mom. Unwilling to go into details, I explained that it had all been a mistake and that everything was copacetic now. She seemed disappointed but I couldn't tell for sure. She did remind me, however, that I should get to my Christmas shopping, and no can opener either.

She didn't ask me what I wanted from her, but I hoped that she'd skip the tie or pair of Argyles that had been my usual yuletide gift. Still, the warm socks might come in handy if the Assburn had me in the can for the holidays, supposing that the Llama hadn't given me his gift first. "'Tis the season to be jolly." For some.

Almost as soon as I finished pouring another libation— Mom's calls invariably had this effect on me—the phone rang again. Polish Phil? Not on your sweet petunias. It was my charming ex-wife.

"Back so soon? Didn't like the room? The view didn't suit you? This wasn't the day for serving caviar and filet mignon?"

It had never been difficult for me to figure why our marriage had failed and this call proved no exception. Time had not smoothed her sharp tongue nor added sugar to her vinegary disposition.

"I'm in no mood for this," I said. "What do you want?"

"*I* don't want anything," she snapped. "I just called to remind you not to be late with this month's alimony or you will be in jail for Christmas, New Year's, and any other holiday that you care to celebrate. I've got shopping to do, and I don't want you to louse it up. Besides, my brother Al will be coming to stay here for a few days, and I want to fix the place up real nice."

She might as well have said that the bubonic plague was coming, that's how much I couldn't stand my nogoodnik, do-nothing, rotten former brother-in-law. But I promised that the check would arrive in time: I was too weary for more fighting. Besides, she hung up before I could get in any nasty words.

Another drink—a good stiff one at that—and the next thing I knew it was three in the morning and I was lying fully clothed on the couch. What the hell, I thought, and went back to sleep.

19

I woke up around 8:30 with a hangover the size of Mae West's chest and with the feeling that Busby Berkeley's dancers were practicing their high kicks inside my head. I was in no condition to go to the office. I was, in fact, in no condition to go anywhere except to the john.

A long shower, a couple of aspirins, and several cups of java helped clear some of the cobwebs and tone down the Berkeley chorines. But I still had no head or heart for the office. It was 10:00 by this time, so I figured that Dotty was there, probably mesmerized by Moby Dick's sperm output.

When she picked up the phone I said that it was Captain Ahab calling. She asked if that was some kind of a joke. Rather than deny or acknowledge it, I told her that it was her boss and that I wouldn't be in for the day, but that she should let me know at home if someone called the office. She said she wasn't clear if she should call me at my home or call me from her home after work. I patiently explained that she should call me at my home but that if I weren't at home before she left the office, she should call me this evening from her home. Then she asked what she should do if I weren't home in the evening. By this time the Berkeley dancers had returned from their coffee break and my blood pressure was somewhere high in the sky searching for Amelia Earhart.

"Dotty," I sighed, "just call as soon as I get any call. Okay?"

"You got it, Mr. D."

I was about to hang up when she asked if I meant that she should let me know about any calls from now on or about the call that came fifteen minutes before I called her. Because if I meant that call, there was a man with a funny sounding Polish name.

The Berkeley dancers were increasing the tempo. "What's his name, Dotty, and did he leave his number?" I yelled.

Sure enough, it was Phil and he had been calling from home. Before hanging up, I told Dotty to call me at any time if another call or calls came in. I hung up before having to go into another exhausting explanation. Then I dialed Phil's number.

"The Mazurki residence. To whom do you wish to speak?"

Once again I had reached Emily Post in drag. I told him that I wanted to speak with Phil.

"Just one moment, if you please, and I'll see if Mr. Mazurki is available." I could hear him tell "Philip" that a gentleman was calling and wished to have words with him. "Yeah, whatta you want," growled a voice.

"Hey, Phil, long time no see. This is Dick DeWitt returning your call."

"Hey, Dickie boy, how ya doing?"

"Hanging in there, Phil, but I've got some problems and I thought maybe you could help me sort them out.

"I'll do my best, my friend. Shoot."

That wasn't the most comforting choice of a word in light of what I feared from the Llama, but what could I expect from a former flatfoot?

"It's complicated," I said. "You got time now?"

"Naw, I gotta take Louie to get a bra and panties . . . . Hello? Hello? You still there, Dick?"

I didn't want to ask or to know about Phil's new taste in his love life. "Sure, I just had something caught in my throat. Ah . . . well maybe we can meet somewhere and talk about the problems."

"Great idea. Let's have lunch today around 1:00. You remember the fish place near the river we used to frequent? What was it called? Oh yeah. 'Mackerel Mike's Fish & Bait'. It sure wasn't fancy, but the grub was decent and cheap, too. That was my favorite joint."

"I remember it, Phil. I'll see you there this afternoon around one." I didn't bother saying that I had read that Mackerel Mike's had been closed twice over the past year for reasons of health code violations. But fighting off a filthy fish paled before my other concerns, and I needed all the help I could get.

I fiddled around the apartment for a while, threw on some comfortable clothes, and took the bus to Mackerel Mike's. The place hadn't changed much. It needed a paint job on the outside and wholesale renovation on the inside. A closer look convinced me that it needed to be razed and let someone other than Mackerel Mike take charge of building a new establishment. Let's put it this way: the Jaded Pavilion, where the chink had been killed, looked like a five-star restaurant compared to this eyesore.

But before I could fully regret having agreed to lunch in this dive, I saw Polish Phil waving his paws at me from a table at the back of the room.

The Polack was a big guy. No, huge, I'd say, although it was quickly apparent that flab had t.k.o.'d muscle. His mug was ugly as ever, and his hair had started to gray, although I had long guessed that a good dye job had prevented the change when he was on the force. But his smile was as broad as ever and he seemed truly glad to see me.

"Hey there, Dickie, sit down and take a load off your number tens," he said, giving me a handshake that showed flab had not conquered all.

We made small talk and ordered lunch from a waiter whose apron had once been white but which now looked as if some deranged artist had used it for a palette. Phil, whose fearlessness and appetite, unlike his honesty, were never in question, ordered a shrimp cocktail, a bowl of Manhattan clam chowder, and a plate of surf and turf. How he could eat that much for lunch I couldn't figure. How a retired cop could afford that much for lunch I didn't want to figure. As for me, I settled for a simple dish of fish and chips. We polished off our orders—we should have polished off the filthy plates on which they came as well. Phil belched and said the food was the same as he remembered. I agreed that the food hadn't changed. I didn't add that my fish tasted as if it had been caught some time when Phil had been on the force. No better were the fries, which were drenched with oil probably syphoned from a Ford that either Mackerel Mike or one of his waiters drove. But I had had worse meals. Or at least I thought I had.

We ordered coffee and got down to business. I filled him in on my troubles with both the Black Llama and Lieutenant Ashburn and his hairy-knuckled subordinates. Phil nodded from time to time that he understood and used a toothpick to mine the remainders of the meal lurking in his tobacco-stained teeth. When I finished with my tale of woe, he looked hard at me for about thirty seconds. "You got big problems, pal," he said, and then resumed excavating the morsels of seafood. For this I had schlepped out here to the riverfront and risked my health, if not my life, eating what passed for food.

"But all's not lost. Gimme some time to think things over and see what we can do about them. Now I gotta get back and do some chores for Louie." And with that he summoned the waiter to bring the bill, insisting that it was his treat. Polish Phil was always a sport.

I took a bus back to the office. I expected to find Dotty in a hot embrace with Moby Dick, but she was busy making up her Christmas list for gifts and cards. That reminded me that I had to get started on mine: a gift for Mom and Dotty, a few cards here and there. A pain in the ass, but aren't all holidays? No calls or visitors came in. The nice money that my chump client Uneeda Baker had given me for the Mona Tuvachevsky-Smith case was fast disappearing. So, I feared, was my life as a free, white, and considerably more than twenty-one-year-old man. Yeah, let's hear it for the holidays. I said an early "so long" to Dotty and left the office around 3:30.

I grabbed some shut-eye at home, fixed some leftovers for supper, and, deciding to look on the bright side of things, headed for The Slippery Elbow. Quiet night there. Asked Gus the bartender for a Jack Daniel's and sat there thinking gloomy thoughts. Gardenia Gertie came over and threw her arms around me and kissed my cheek. Swell, I thought, now I'm going to get a disease on top of everything else. On my way to the gent's room, I saw Hyman the Hebe sitting in a corner by himself and looking as if he had lost his last bagel. Chatted for a few minutes and learned that the feds were investigating him for some alleged fancy accounting maneuvers. On top of that his wife, Yetta, had found out about his girlfriend. I guessed the poor schnook was not going to have a good Hanukkah. After the men's room, I headed home.

I hoped a good night's sleep would help. Instead, I woke screaming from a dream where Polish Phil, wearing bra and panties, was chasing me down a street. I turned the corner to escape but ran into the Llama, the Assburn, O'Meara and Bruttafaccia, all four of whom drew their guns and began firing at me. Happy holidays to one and all.

20

A raw December wind was nipping at me as I headed downtown to the office. No snow, fortunately, but I was toting my galoshes just in case. Mom had always warned me that wet feet were the devil's companion. I still hadn't figured out what that meant, but I had enough trouble on my hands. So, too, apparently did the city. A glimpse at the newspaper headlines at a corner stand informed me that violent crimes were on the rise. I wondered if I would soon be contributing to the statistics.

Too tired to walk the eight flights to my office, I waited for the elevator.

"Morning, Mr. DeWitt. Howzit goin'?"

Nine-thirty and Joe was smashed already. His breath smelled like a combo dinner of sour pickles and marinated herring.

"Fine, Joe," I said, edging back into the recesses of the lift.

"Have a good one, Mr. DeWitt," he said as I got off at my floor. "And, say, have a Merry Christmas, too." Drunk or not, he was waiting for his gift.

"Mr. D, you look awful!" were Dotty's first words as I opened the door to the office.

"Yeah, I know. Didn't sleep well, but I'll be fine."

94

"I hope so. You don't want to be sick for the holidays, do you?"

If Joe and Dotty don't stop reminding me of the coming festivities, I thought, I'm going to make sure that they don't live to enjoy theirs.

A cup of coffee whipped up by Dotty the dispenser of good cheer helped to improve my mood, though barely.

Half an hour later someone knocked on the door. "Come in," I said, grabbing my .38.

He was short and slender. Beady eyes, a sharply pointed nose, and a pencil-thin black mustache dominated his tan face. He was sporting a vicuna coat, which looked new and expensive. He seemed tense and kept looking around. Maybe the holidays were also getting to him.

Have a seat, I told him, and asked him what he had on his mind. He immediately took off his hat and coat. He told me that he suspected that his wife was having an affair with a pool hall shark who was at least twenty years her junior. She was a "*puta*," he said. I made a note to look up the word later. Meanwhile, I couldn't figure out his accent. It sounded familiar, but in a city this size . . .

Tell me, Mr., er Mr. . . . . "

He looked more nervous. "My name is John Doe," he stammered.

Well, you needn't ask if that got my attention. Anyone with the name "Dough" was not to be dismissed. With bills coming in, I was not about to let him and his vicuna coat escape.

"I'll need some information and, of course, a photo of your wife. Then I'll get right on the case. You've come to the right place, Mr. Dough."

At which point my mustachioed meal ticket leaped from his seat, grabbed his coat and hat, and promised that he'd return.

"Where are you going?" I asked, trying to keep a sense of alarm and cruel disappointment from my voice. But it was useless. He was out the door before I could race across the room and bar his way.

"That wasn't very nice what he did," Dotty said.

"Just shut up, Dotty, and go back to *Moby Dick*."

"Oh, I finished that last night. I've just started *The Idiot*, by that Russian with that Russian-sounding name. You know him."

I said I didn't know him and refrained from asking my idiot why she was reading about his idiot.

I didn't have to wait long for the second annoying visitor, or, in this case, visitors, who burst through the door before I could reach for my rod.

"Well, well, well," I said, "if it isn't detectives ugly and uglier. What do King Kong and Mighty Giuseppe Young want today? Looking for a few stale donuts?"

"Shut up, smartass," O'Meara snapped. "We're here to make nice with you. Of course if you prefer," he glanced at his sour-looking partner, "we could take you down to the station and play some Christmas tunes on your thick skull. Tony here can play a nightstick sweeter than that spade Lionel Hampton plays the vibes. Wanna go for a demonstration?"

"Okay, O'Meara. To what do I owe the pleasure of seeing your two pusses?"

O'Meara, whose voice usually carried from Maine to Missouri, bent down to where I was sitting and said quietly, "Get rid of the one with the big tits first."

I was tempted to ask, but didn't, if he meant Holy Canoli. I settled for, "Why?"

"Because, dummy, my partner and I have something that you'll want to hear."

The only thing that I could imagine wanting to hear from these two Neanderthals was that they were quitting the force or, better yet, going to Sing Sing for the next few decades. For all I knew, the Ripper and the Canoli were going to beat the living bejesus out of me once my secretary left. Still, beggars can't be choosy, as they say, although I recall one sitting on a park bench who complained when I gave him only a nickel. I guess he learned his lesson when I took back my nickel and the other coins from his tin cup.

"Dotty," I said, "why don't you take a little stroll around the block for the next ten or fifteen minutes?"

She looked up from her reading. "But my feet hurt, Mr. D, and what's more, I haven't found out who the idiot is in my book."

"Dotty," I sighed, "just go out. I promise you that at least one idiot will still be here when you get back. Besides," I added, looking at O'Meara and Bruttafaccia, "I can detect a bad smell in here."

"Well it's certainly not me!" Dotty exclaimed. In no time flat she grabbed her hat and coat and left, giving the door a good slam and the three of us a dirty look.

O'Meara asked where I found her and how I put up with her. She's got a great chest, he said, but the brains of a dodo. I told him that I won a raffle at the College of Hard Knockers and hard knockers were hard to come by these days.

"You got a great sense of humor, DeWitt. Hasn't he, Tony?"

"Yeah, he's a riot, John. They're gonna love him up in Attica."

"He ain't going to Attica if he plays his cards right." The Ripper gave me a smile like the one Roosevelt must have had when he won the last election. "You know, Diamond, we could get you for killing that chink. Right now it doesn't look too good for you. But you know, strange things have a way of happening."

"Like what, for instance?"

"Oh, I don't know." He looked up at the ceiling and pondered for a moment. "Like maybe that chopstick and plate that have your prints all over disappearing." He smiled the smile of corruption unleashed. "That evidence room at the Precinct is a mess. Things tend to get misplaced, don't they, Tony?"

The Canoli's mouth was full of a sticky candy bar, so he gave a grunt and a nod.

"And naturally we have some clout with Lieutenant Ashburn, who really isn't such a bad egg once you get to know him." The Ripper gave me his biggest smile yet. "Are you getting my drift, my friend?"

I wasn't his friend and the only drift I was getting was that of two stinking coppers on the take. The air was smelling worse than before Dotty left.

"Does this drift have a price, O'Meara, or are you feeling especially generous at holiday time?"

"For you, I'm always feeling generous." Then his gaze hardened into pure malice and contempt. "And since both the Canoli and I are in the Christmas spirit of giving but also getting, we'll square things for you for a small sum, say a C-note. Naturally that's a C-note apiece."

I felt like pulling out my .38 and doing the world a favor. But I realized that the only favor I could do was for myself in this pitiless world we live in.

"I need some time to think about it, O'Meara."

"Sure," he smiled, "take your time." Then he turned to his partner and asked how many more shopping days to Christmas.

"Not many, John, and we got a lot of shopping to do."

O'Meara reached across the desk and yanked me up by my shirt front. "You got forty-eight hours to accept our generous offer, gumshoe. Take it or leave it."

End of conversation. End of visit by two of the city's most corrupt. End of my semi-clean shirt, which O'Meara had soiled with his filthy paw.

I didn't know what I was going to do. I didn't want to grease the palms of these two creeps, and even if I agreed to do so, I wasn't sure my bank account would let me. Nor could I be sure that these two rats wouldn't just take the money and then do nothing and deny that they had ever made me an offer. On the other hand, I wasn't making any progress toward clearing my name. For no good reason I walked over to Dotty's desk and began leafing through her book. After several pages I concluded that the hero, Prince Mishegas, or something like that, wasn't doing too well either.

Dotty returned, still pouting. I let her pout. Serves anyone right who bothers with Russian novels.

I was ready to knock off early when the phone rang. Dotty reluctantly answered it and said it was a Phil Mazurka. I don't know if she was trying to be funny or merely being her customary self, but I was glad to hear from the Polack in any case. It turned out that he hadn't yet uncovered any useful news but he had his feelers out and was sure that something would break. I figured that it would be only my head that would break but kept that disturbing thought to myself.

"Anyway, Dickie boy, you need some cheering up and so Louie and I want you to come over for a special meal tomorrow night. Louie's just dying to meet you. Practically swooned when I described you."

"I can hardly wait," I told him after a few seconds.

"Louie can't either," came the response.

Mr. Dough, O'Meara and Bruttafaccia, and Louie. Some guys have all the luck; I'd be willing to share mine. I said good night to Dotty, who barely looked up from her book to mumble some words I didn't catch. Then I left. By the time I was halfway home I realized that I had forgotten my galoshes. With my luck there'd be a blizzard by tomorrow.

21

The next twenty-four hours got me nowhere. I went home, had a few snorts, fixed a peanut butter and tongue sandwich, and went to bed earlier than I had in years. Slept long but badly and refused to go to the office in the morning. Didn't want to face Dotty and her nonsense. Meanwhile I saw no light shining at the end of my dark tunnel, no solutions to my problems either with the coppers or the Llama. I paced back and forth in my apartment like a trapped rat. Then I went out to a neighborhood smoke shop, where I nearly bought a pack of Old Golds. I had quit smoking a few years ago when my wife—she wasn't my ex yet—said I was smelling up our place with my cigarettes and that either I give up my filthy habit or she'd leave me. Surprise. I quit and a month later she ordered me out. I probably would have gone back to the fags had I not heard a rumor that smoking could ruin your health and send you to an early appointment with the Grim Reaper. Don't know why I paid attention to that dumbass rumor started by one quack or another, but even today at the smoke shop I couldn't bring myself to ask for my former standbys. Sadie Plotz called in the early afternoon to ask whether the police's trail on the Llama was getting hot and if I wanted to come to her place this evening to discuss it. The trail might not be hot but Sadie sure was.

Told her that the trail was cold and that I had a cold but would be in touch soon.

Maybe what was putting me on edge even more than the threats of the Llama and the police was the prospect of dinner at Polish Phil's and meeting Louie. Hell, I had no beef with perverts, but if that faggot Louie put just one of his pansy paws on me, if he lisped just once into my ear . . . Cut it out, I told myself. You'll go there, hear if Phil has any more news, and be polite to his boyfriend.

I dressed conservatively for the evening get-together: dark suit, white shirt, nearly-stainless red tie. Didn't want to inflame Louie unnecessarily or give him the wrong idea. I stopped at a liquor store on the way to the bus stop. Knowing that Phil was a big fan of anything and everything Polish, I splurged and bought a pint of Polish vodka, which the clerk swore was pure Polish despite its label that said, "distilled in Whippany, New Jersey." Whippany or Warsaw, it didn't matter that much.

Phil lived in a fancy part of town, which befit someone who had cleaned up on the job. Never mind stocks or real estate or rich relatives. If you knew which side was up and where it was at, as a copper you could make a bundle. And Phil had. I wondered if his shady path and past had ever crossed with those of the Assburn and his two associates, the mick and the dago.

I gave the fancily clad doorman my name. He told me Mr. Mazurki was expecting me and to go right up to the top floor. The elevator man, wearing similar garb, greeted me effusively and hoisted me to the Polack's pad twenty-two floors above terra firma. I rang the buzzer, wondering whether Phil or his sweetie would answer.

"Hey, Dickie boy, it's swell to see you. Come on in. Let me show you around the joint," he said as he pumped my hand until it hurt. "Louie's in the kitchen fixing chow but is almost finished."

The "joint" contained a large living room, dining area, and two rooms, probably bedrooms, their doors closed. The furniture seemed prewar and comfortable. As I suspected,

Phil was not big on decorations, but two stood out: a knight in shining armor, to which was Scotch-taped his old police badge, and an armadillo stuffed and mounted on the wall. I asked where he got the latter, and he said it was a gift from Dilly Farkas. (I hadn't been aware that he knew Dilly, but then Phil had made it his business to know a lot of people.). But the highlight of the apartment was a terrace that overlooked the river. Phil said that he liked sitting out there and thinking about all the bodies that were swimming with the fishes. He said that no matter how down he felt, that always cheered him up.

"Dinner's ready, fellows."

Louie had a pleasing voice, I had to say, his laryngitis or cold having disappeared. But it would have sounded a helluva lot better coming from a dame.

"I hope you like it."

Jumping Jehoshaphat, or whoever's jumping these days. The voice *did* belong to a dame. He was a she, and a real stunner at that.

"Dickie DeWitt, meet Louie Prima," Phil said.

"Oh, Phil, I wish you would call me 'Louise'. You know that's my real name. And just because you think it's cute to give me the same name as that musician . . . "

"Yeah, I know, doll, but I like to introduce you as 'Louie' and catch the take on faces like Dickie's. Did you notice how when he saw you come out of the kitchen his jaw dropped almost to his dickey?"

Phil laughed like a hyena at his joke, Louie blushed, and I just kept staring at the best-looking woman I had seen since Jean Harlow's last movie.

We sat down to eat. Louie, or Louise, as she asked me to call her, sure knew how to fix a meal: steak, potatoes, brussels sprouts, cake and ice cream, coffee, the works. I was itching to know all about her and the Polack but figured this wasn't the time or place. So I asked innocent questions: Where are you from? What do you do? What do you like? Turns out she was from Chicago, visiting New York for an indefinite stay. She was cagey about what she did, noting vaguely that it had something to do with the arts. As for what she liked, she turned her big blue ones toward Phil and said, "He's what I like." The Polack belched and beamed the brightest smile I've seen since Roosevelt turned Alf Landon into chopped liver.

After dinner Louise excused herself and said that she'd see to the dishes while we boys had our little boys' talk. I asked if she needed help bringing things into the kitchen, but she said that that was a woman's job. Louise was definitely my kind of woman.

Phil and I left the table, went into the living room, and settled into matching wing chairs. Phil asked what I wanted to drink. He poured me a Jack Daniel's and for himself some of the vodka I had brought. I took mine with ice, he took his neat. "Hey, this is real Polish vodka," he said after a couple of sips. I was glad that "Whippany, New Jersey" was in very fine print.

"So, let's see what we've got," he said. "First, I'm sure you heard the good news that you're off the hook for the killing of the chink."

I figured that either my hearing had lost a few hundred decibels or Phil had spiked my Jack Daniel's. When I recovered my speech, I told him that I had heard no such thing and recounted the extortion demands that O'Meara and Bruttafaccia had made yesterday.

Phil frowned and began to crack his oversized knuckles. "You mean to say that the mick and the guinea tried to hit on you when they already knew that you were in the clear? I've seen some crooked cops in my day, but those two go to the top of the list. A slant-eye who was the cook in the restaurant witnessed the murder of the waiter and came in and told Assburn two nights ago. He claimed that a man with a thin mustache and funny accent had slipped poison into the waiter's chow mein while he, the cook, was watching. The man told him that he'd better keep his trap shut or he'd be sorry. I guess the cook's conscience got the better of him." Phil downed some more of Whippany's finest. "And I guess Assburn told O'Meara and Bruttafaccia before they paid you a visit. I bet that he was in for a kickback if his pals were successful with you. I wouldn't mind sitting on my patio some nice evening and watching their bodies drift by." Rumors had it over the years that at least a few of the bodies that floated by Phil's apartment had been compliments of Phil himself or some of his closest buddies. I never asked. He never told.

"I don't know how you found all this out, Phil, but it's a big load off my mind and shoulders."

"I still got friends in the department, pal, and I'm real glad you're home free. Now if you need help with those two mugs who're trying to hit you up . . . "

"Thanks, Phil, I think I can handle them, but what about the Black Llama? Anything happening on that front?"

Phil refreshed my drink and his. "Nothing definite yet, Dickie, but I've got feelers out and an idea or two. Soon. Soon."

I could tell that the subject had reached a dead end. Phil would be in touch when and if matters began to gel. Meanwhile, it was getting late. We shmoozed a bit about old times and then I left, but not before thanking him and telling him to thank Louise for me. I had hoped to see Louise after she finished her work in the kitchen, but she had disappeared. I was disappointed, more so than I would have guessed. There was something about her that I couldn't let go of. Stop it, you ungrateful bastard, I told myself, she's the Polack's squeeze.

22

I slept well that night. True, the Llama was still lurking somewhere out there and eager to get me, but at least the two suits from the 13th Precinct and their boss would no longer be on my back. Half a loaf is better than none any day.

Even the weather had taken a nice turn. Seasonably cold but sunny and no hint of the white stuff. I walked to work, whistling a few catchy tunes that I had caught over the years. Life's no bowl of cherries, that's for sure, but it does have its days.

I bounded up a few flights of stairs and then walked up the rest of the way. The landlord still hadn't fixed my sign but that was a small matter for now. "Hi ya, cutie," I said to Dotty as I entered the office. Trouble was she wasn't there. Did some guy get lucky with her last night or was she too engrossed in her latest Russian novel. Maybe they're still in bed together reading about Prince Mishegas. I'd sure like to be in the sack right now with a certain gorgeous woman who has a man's name, although I'd skip the book for something more to my taste. I felt a little ashamed that I was doing this with Phil's girl even if it was only in my mind. But not ashamed enough to stop.

A knock on the door disturbed my lewd thoughts and brought me back to the real world. I grabbed my gun and said come in. The saintly enforcers of law and order had once again darkened my door and my thoughts.

"Well, well, well," I said. "If it isn't the bad news buffoons. What can I do for you fine upstanding gentlemen?"

"You can cut the crap, for one thing, and you can learn some respect for your betters for another. Ain't that right, Tony?"

The Canoli was too occupied with trying to hold an ice cream cone in one hand and rub some of it from his suit with the other to do more than make an animal-like noise.

The muscles around my jaw tightened. "Are you Alley Oops here for another try at shaking me down, even though you know I had nothing to do with the waiter's death?" The goons looked at one another. "Oh yeah," I said, "word's out about how the cook came in and spilled the beans, or whatever a chink cook spills. Didn't think I'd find out, did you? You guys make me sick. Now get out of here and try breaking some other poor guy's balls."

Expecting one or both of them to try some heavy-handed stuff with me, I yanked open my desk drawer and slipped on my brass knuckles. Imagine my surprise when O'Meara gave me a big smile.

"Ah, come on, Mr. DeWitt, you got us all wrong. We only came over to let you know that the cook was snuffed out last night. Someone didn't like his egg foo yung and slit his throat with a straight razor. You wouldn't know anything about that, would you?"

My blood, which had been boiling, froze. My alibi had gone down the drain with the chink's blood. Back to square one, where the cops could claim that I wasn't the innocent I declared myself to be. Sure, it made no sense that I would have offed the guy who put me in the clear by saying someone else killed the waiter. But the city's finest always want to solve murders and they don't much care if they pin the rap on an innocent slob, especially if they have it in for the slob to begin with.

"Come on, O'Meara, why would I kill the guy who could establish my innocence? Does that make sense to you and the Canoli?"

O'Meara smirked and fixed his tie, smudging some recently acquired jam in the process. "We're just doing our job, buddy boy. We're not saying you did in one or both of the chinks, but we got to keep an open mind on the subject. Of course we could still try to put in a few good words for you with the Lieutenant, but that's up to you, if you get my point."

I got his point, all right, and it was aimed directly at the cowhide wallet my ex had given me for my birthday a few centuries back. Now I had to worry about the coppers again. I told O'Meara and Bruttafaccia that I didn't need, didn't want, their good words with the Assburn, and that they should scram and let an honest private eye do an honest day's work. That brought some guffaws from the duo, but they did leave.

I was wondering whether Polish Phil had learned about this recent unpleasant turn of events, and I was thinking of calling him when the phone rang.

"Hello, Señor DeWitt," the heavily accented voice said, "this is John Doe. You remember me from yesterday?"

Well at least some business is heading my way. "Sure thing, Mr. Dough. Say the word and I'm ready to get on the case and find out if your missus has been doing more than shooting for the corner pockets down at the pool hall."

"No, Señor DeWitt, I do not have a señora, and if I did, I wouldn't let the *puta* go near a pool hall. What do you take me for, eh?"

Why is this jokester trying to pull my chain, I wondered. "I don't understand, Mr. Dough, why you came here yesterday or why you're calling me today if you don't want me to do a job for you." I hadn't let my voice betray the fact that I wanted to have a go at his face and send him to his dentist for dentures, both upper and lower.

"Now pay attention, you stupid *gringo*. Look around your office. Anything missing?"

I took my time looking but didn't see anything unusual. "There's nothing missing as far as I can tell," I told him, "and I don't cotton to being called names. Got me, spic?"

"Oh, I got you all right, Señor Gringo. And we got your little *chiquita*, too."

I didn't know what "chiquita" meant, but I had a pretty good idea he was referring to the size of my you-know-what. I checked to be sure, but it was still there.

"Listen, taco head, mine is bigger than yours any day of the week, and so are my frijoles. Get what I mean?"

The palavering ceased. "*Si*, I get what you mean. Now you get what I mean, and get it right or you'll be a sorry *hombre*. We've got your secretary."

I looked around the room once more to make sure that I had not overlooked Dotty or that she had not just come in and I had failed to see her. I was shocked. Why would anyone want her, I wondered. She's a babe, all right, but she can't type worth a fig and she drives you bananas with her fancy books. But what really shocks me is that she would quit without giving notice. If Dotty has anything going for her—besides a body that many a man would go to the electric chair for with a smile on his face—it was her loyalty. How could she do this to me?

"Listen," I told the lowlife at the other end of the line, "you're a rat for stealing my secretary from me before she even had the decency to give two-weeks' notice. But she's a good girl, and I hope that you'll treat her right and pay her a decent wage." In my heart I knew I'd miss Dotty and wished her all the best.

"Listen yourself, Señor Bird Brain. We have taken your secretary and we will kill her unless you do as you're told. *Comprende?*"

Wait a minute. Now it was becoming clear. Why those dirty bastards. They'd kidnapped my Dotty!

"You can't do this," I shouted. "There's a law against kidnapping. Ever hear of the Lindbergh law, knucklehead? The chair's waiting for you unless you let her go right now." I hoped that this would convince him. It didn't.

"We'll call you Monday at the same time, Señor Snoop, with our demands. Don't worry about the lovely *señorita*, at least not until then. And you have a very good day. *Hasta mañana*." Click.

They say that the sure way to kayo an opponent is to hit him hard with the old left-right combination. I felt as if Señor Dough and the police had walloped me with that lethal combination, and I was staggering. My knees were buckling, but I hadn't hit the canvas. At least not yet. I thought matters over. Then I called Phil and informed him of the dirty substance that had hit the fan.

"Take it easy, Dickie boy. I happen to know for a fact that Assburn and his henchmen can't pin anything on you even if the cook was killed. You see, a pal of mine heard the cook's story when he came in the station. He's not going to forget it either, not the way he feels about the Lieutenant and his goons."

That was the good news.

"What about Dotty?"

That was the not-so-good news.

"I don't know, pal. I'm going to be frank with you. It doesn't sound good. But keep cool. You aren't going to know what the scumbags want until they contact you. It certainly sounds like this Mr. Doe is in cahoots with the Llama. I'd go to the bank on that one. Listen, I still got my feelers out, and maybe something will break later today. I'll call you soon as I hear anything. By the way, Louie said she really enjoyed meeting you. What a gal, don't you think?"

Yeah, what a gal. I'd be all smiles after hearing her compliment, but I was too concerned about the other gal, my Gal Friday. But the Polack was right: I couldn't do anything for now. And on that note I closed up shop and headed home. The only catchy ditty I could think of whistling en route was Irving Berlin's "What'll I Do?" Yeah, what do I do?

23

I dragged myself home, feeling like Max Schmeling must have felt when Joe Louis beat the living tar out of him during their rematch. I hadn't felt this bad since my wife, some years back, had said that her brother was out of work and would stay with us for a few weeks. (The lazy bastard stayed eight months. I was sorely tempted to put it to my wife that either he left or I would. In retrospect, I would have come out way ahead if I had.) Poor Dotty. My mind raced with thoughts of what the Llama and John Dough were doing to her right now—taunting her, molesting her, depriving her of her novels. I had to save her. Sure. But how? I don't believe in miracles, especially after having had my 30-to-1 longshot nag miss winning a big one by a nose at Aqueduct. And sitting on my slightly overweight butt wasn't going to save her either. What kind of gumshoe, I thought, drags his ass on his own case? So after a skimpy supper of Spam, canned hash, and sugar-coated peanuts, I got moving.

The Elbow seemed as morose as me. Several of the gang were on hand. Southpaw Sammy Stickit had tears in his eyes and was telling a couple of new faces how he could have been a contender for the major leagues if a lousy umpire hadn't got him banned from professional baseball. And what was he now, he lamented? A longshoreman. Gardenia Gertie

110

also had tears in her eyes. She had her arms draped around the neck of poor Hyman the Hebe, who was blubbering like a baby. If Gertie got any closer he was going to have a lot more to blubber about. And even Gus the bartender looked more downcast than usual. His mother-in-law, I discovered, was about to pay him and his wife a visit for an indefinite period. The wife, it seems, had informed him that he would have to sleep on the couch.

But at least Light Fingers Louie was in a jovial mood. "Hi there, Mr. DeWitt. Long time, no see."

It hadn't been a long time at all, but I let that pass and asked why he was beaming from lopsided ear to lopsided ear.

Louie looked around and then whispered that he was in on something big. I told him that if he didn't watch his step the only thing big that he'd find himself in would have bars and be under the supervision of a warden. I reminded him that since he had done time before, the law would bear that in mind if he got in trouble again.

"Don't worry, Mr. DeWitt, I'll watch my step. He took a swig of the watery beer he was drinking and asked how I'd been doing. I told him what had happened to Dotty.

"Geez, that's awful," he said. "You want me to nose about and see if I can learn anything?"

Not a bad idea, I thought. Not necessarily a good one either, but at this juncture I needed all the help I could find. I told him yes and treated him to another watery beer. Then I walked over to tell Hyman to keep his chin up. That made him cry harder. Gertie was touched by what she called my act of kindness and planted a big smacker on my mouth. I wanted to cry, too, for fear that a social disease was about to pay me an unsolicited visit. Needless to say, my subsequent night's sleep was none too good. A dream that had the Llama and the pencil-thin mustache stuffing pages of novels down Dotty's throat didn't help. Nor did the phone ringing. I reached under the sheet and grabbed the receiver. "What creep is calling me in the middle of the night and what does the creep want?"

"Sorry, Mr. DeWitt, but I might have something useful about this Black Llama guy, and you told me to ring you up anytime."

I didn't recall saying this to Louie, but if he had any news about the Llama I didn't mind the three a.m. reveille.

Louie, it seems, had run into a spic by the name of Julio Valdez, who used to run with the Llama but left his gang after some dispute and who currently was doing some things that Louie would rather not mention. Louie told me that Valdez took his breakfast daily between 8:00 and 9:00 at the Cinco Hombres, a greasy spoon run by four brothers. I thanked Louie for the tip and promised him a couple of drinks next time I saw him at the Elbow. I figured I was safe in making the promise since Louie didn't dare show his ugly puss in his regular haunts very often for fear the cops would find him. I also figured that I'd go look for Valdez the following morning. Hell, it was morning already.

The Cinco Hombres was located in the middle of Spictown, where I wouldn't want to be found at night unless accompanied by General MacArthur and whatever troops he's commanding. The diner, like the rest of the area, was so rundown that you'd need to climb a stepladder to see street level. There was what I guessed to be a menu in the window but I couldn't read it, not because I didn't know Spanish— which was true enough—but because the windows were dirtier than Gardenia Gertie's underwear. Hell, I couldn't even make out who was inside the diner.

Inside, however, things got better. The smell of good Latino cooking knocked my socks off, although I was still wearing both of them when I looked down. The diner was pretty crowded. I didn't have a clue if Valdez was one of the clientele, and if so, which one he was. There was a hot-looking dish sitting on a stool and tending to the cash register. I figured she knew how to count or counted with the boss. In either case she was probably bright enough to finger Valdez for me. All it would take would be some of my vaulted charm.

"*Buenos dias*, cutie. Are you one of the Cinco Hombres?"

She gave me a look that told me she wasn't, but I persisted. "If Señor Valdez is here," I told her, "there's something in it for you."

Her eyes brightened as she smiled and nodded toward a corner of the diner. "Sí, *señor gringo*, he's the one sitting by himself next to the mop and pail full of feelthy water."

"Thanks, cutie. Here's a little something for your help," I said, handing her a nickel. "And say 'hello' to the other hombres for me."

I strolled over to Valdez, looked him in the eye, and knocked over the mop and pail. I could tell he wasn't pleased as he began wringing out his pants cuff and shaking water from his sandals.

"Sorry about that, Mr. Valdez, but accidents happen."

He looked at me. "And especially with you, I bet. Anyway, who are you and what can I do for you?"

I sat down uninvited and introduced myself. I told him that Light Fingers Louie said he knew Miguel Malvado, aka the Black Llama, and that maybe he could give me a lead on him.

"Maybe, maybe not," he said as he slurped down his Wheaties topped with sliced black beans and jalapeño peppers. "Why you want to know?"

I told him what a vicious, dangerous scumbag the Llama was and what danger he presented to society. I had to find him, I explained, or who knows what dastardly deed he'd next commit.

"Look, señor, I know what a bastard the Llama is. I was a bastard, too, before I saw—how you say?—the light.

I asked what light he saw and at what intersection. He told me that it was none of my *norteamericano* business.

"Look, señor, I don't know where the Llama and his amigos are, but I can tell you something about him and maybe that will help you. And maybe that will help me, too," he said, rubbing the fingertips of his right hand.

"Look, Mr. Valdez, I don't see how that's going to help your itchy fingers. But if it's a simple rash or even eczema, I can tell you what helped my cousin Anatole. He suffered a bad rash and itched constantly until one of his bowling partners told him about . . . "

"Listen to me, Señor Dimwit, if you want my help it will cost you *mucho dinero. Comprende?*

I understood, and we negotiated. He drove a hard bargain and asked for a fin. I drove a harder one. I jewed him down to two bucks and a promise to dry his sandals with my handkerchief. The joke was on him since my snot rag was filthier than his footwear.

"Let me ask you, what do you already know about the Llama, Señor Dimwit?"

I told him how Mona had told me his name and said that he was a defrocked priest who had taught her calculus.

Valdez roared with laughter, spewing his Wheaties in my face. I had begun to work on his sandals with my handkerchief and so I had to use my tie to wipe my face. He asked me why I hadn't used one of the napkins that filled a metal holder on the table. That was a good idea, but I hadn't thought of it. I told him to mind his own business and get on with what he knew about the Llama.

"First of all, this Señorita Mona, either she not know all the facts or she lying to you." He smiled and wiped his lips with several strands of the oily black hair that hung down the side of his face. "True, his name is Miguel Malvado. Whether he taught her calculus I could not say since I haven't seen him in years. But as for his being a defrocked priest? No way. He was the son of the devil, that one." He interrupted his story to order another bowl of Wheaties with the usual black beans and jalapeño peppers. "Only this time put some cheese on, *carita*," he yelled to the waitress.

"Now where was I? Oh, *sí*, I remember. The Llama, as you probably guessed, is from Peru. The Andes. You know them? Trouble always found him and he found it when it didn't find him. He and a few friends used to guide wealthy *turistas* to see Machu Picchu. Some of these visitors never came back. They fell into the valley or simply disappeared, he told authorities. No one could say otherwise. Meanwhile he had become the richest man in the village and married the prettiest señorita. That's when his big trouble started. His young wife told him she was different from the others in the village and that she wasn't going to wear that—what do you call it in English?—that traditional bowler hat that respectable Peruvian women wear. They argued. They hit each other. They argued more. They hit each other more. As you can imagine, the whole village by this time was laughing at Miguel because he could not control his woman. Miguel said nothing. He waited. Then one day his wife disappeared. Miguel reported this to the police and said he would be heartbroken forever if his beautiful, good wife were not found. No one believed this nonsense, of course, but no one could say that he was responsible for her disappearance.

"*Carita*! Some more jalapeños for my Wheaties *por favor*." Valdez dabbed at his lips with his hair.

"Now, señor, here is the best part. Miguel was one greedy bastard, and he cheated his friends of their share of the money they made from robbing tourists. One of them—a very brave man since everyone knew that Miguel had a violent temper—asked for his share. Miguel told him—well, you can imagine what he told him. The man said okay, Miguel, and walked away. The next day the man went to the police and said that Miguel had murdered his wife and chopped her to pieces, which he then fed to a nasty black llama that, because of its color, was not accepted by other llamas. Now no one believed that story either, but Miguel had become so unpopular with the townspeople as well as the police that the latter decided to arrest him. Miguel heard about this, fled the village, and hid deep in the Andes, but not before vowing eternal vengeance. And that, *señor gringo*, is that. Now you know a lot more about the Black Llama."

He was right. Now I did know much more about the Llama: where he was from, how he got his name, and most important, just how cruel and vicious he was. I knew that I had to stop him before he struck again. I thanked Valdez and took a jalapeño from his bowl. "By the way," I asked as I was leaving, "did you know the man who ratted on him to the police?"

Valdez broke into a big grin before he began to laugh uncontrollably. "Yes, I know him very well. You could even say that I know him as well as I know myself."

I didn't get the joke, but Latins have a different sense of humor, I suppose. Anyway, I had more important things to do. Like put out the fire that was burning in my mouth.

24

Sunday was a lost day. I fretted and then I drank. Then I fretted some more, and then I drank some more. I felt like a hamster running on a wheel. Valdez had given me some interesting info on the Llama but no leads for catching up with him.

A cup of strong java and some leftover hash on Monday morning helped a bit, as did a pair of fresh socks and underwear, which I had forgotten to change for several days. I tuned in the radio and learned that the nips were giving the chinks a lot of trouble in Asia and the krauts were doing likewise to the hebes in Germany. What a world! Meanwhile I had my own troubles. I put on my trenchcoat and green fedora and headed for the office, where I expected to hear from Señor John Dough.

I figured I needed to save my energy, and so I waited for the elevator instead of walking up the eight flights. Joe was off today, probably the result of too much booze, and his cousin Billy was standing in for him, as he did when Joe had had too much sauce the night before. Billy, I had learned from Joe, was a teetotaler but had a slight problem with drugs and occasionally hallucinated. I think this was one of those days: he wore different-colored shoes, one white and one brown, and kept asking if I thought President Coolidge was doing a good job. After undershooting and overshooting my floor a few times, he managed to land the elevator. I told him to have a good day. He told me to give his regards to Mr. Coolidge.

Tense with worry like a chicken about to meet a man with a hatchet, I paced my office. The phone rang at 10:17.

"Hello?"

"*Buenos dias*, Señor DeWitt. You are well, yes?"

It was the mustache. I wanted to pluck his upper lip adornment hair by hair and then fry his frijoles, but I kept my calm.

"Where's Dotty, you good-for-nothing, sleazy spic?"

"That is not a very nice way to speak, Señor DeWitt, and I advise you to watch your tongue if you know what's good for the *muchacha*."

It was hard to watch my tongue, especially without a mirror, but I knew I had to.

"Okay, okay. What's the deal?"

"The deal, *señor*, is that you will be so nice as to give us five thousand dollars and we'll give you back the girl." He paused. "And in one piece."

He might as well have asked me to hand over Fort Knox. Five thousand dollars! Who's he kidding? Where does he think I can come up with that sort of moola? Yet I knew he was serious and that Dotty's life was at stake.

"Listen, Mr. Dough, I don't have that kind of money. Where do you expect me to find it? We're in a depression, or haven't you heard?"

"That is your problem, *amigo*," he said. "But I think you'd better solve it if you want to see your pretty little secretary again." There was a pause. "Since we're not unreasonable people we'll give you forty-eight hours." Another pause. "But only forty-eight hours. *Adiós*." Click.

I walked over to the window and looked at the scene below. Christmas decorations brightened stores and beckoned passersby to come in and buy gifts. A small Salvation Army band stood across the street, no doubt playing appropriate tunes and reminding people to give to those less fortunate than themselves. I wondered if Dotty would be alive to celebrate or if she would be among the unfortunate. Poor Dotty. Well, at least I hadn't yet bought her Christmas gift.

The phone rang. I half expected it to be John Dough, hoped that it would be either Polish Phil or Light Fingers Louie with some good news, but was surprised to find that it was Uneeda Baker, whose visit to my office had touched the match to this whole mess.

"Mr. DeWitt, you won't believe it, but I have good news and then wonderful news."

I was sort of glad that the sun was shining for someone these days, especially for this poor sap, whose girlfriend had put him through the wringer.

"Good for you, Mr. Baker," I said. "What's the news?"

"You remember that I had an Uncle Ebeneezer who had left me something? Well, the whole thing got settled and I'm going to get more money than I know what to do with. I'm thinking of opening another bakery and calling it 'Ebeneezer's Eclairs' in honor of my uncle."

"That's wonderful news, Mr. Baker, and I'm really glad to hear it," I lied. "And what's the good news?" I forced myself to ask.

"No, Mr. DeWitt, that's the good news. The wonderful news is that Mona will be out of jail in a few days and then we can resume our beautiful relationship."

If there's a God, I thought, he must reward the hopelessly stupid. Here's this jerk who nearly got himself royally screwed by some tall broad who'd rather play basketball than house, and now he wants her back. And why would she want to go back to this sawed-off moron? Couldn't be Uncle Ebeneezer Baker's spondulicks, could it? Nah. And how in holy hell was Mona getting sprung from the cooler after all the hot water she was in?

"I'm really glad that Mona will go free and that you can have her back, Mr. Baker." I didn't just lie this time, I may have told the whopper to end all whoppers. "But tell me, how did she manage to convince the authorities to let her go?"

I could tell that Baker was wondering whether he should open his yap to me. He started to say something, stopped, started, stopped. Finally he made me promise not to tell a soul how it happened. I promised, and then he explained. First of all, he never believed that Mona was trying to deceive him. It was all the work of that nasty foreigner, who worked his Svengali-like charm on her. He—meaning Baker—didn't want to go on without his elevated damsel, and so he thought hard and long about what he could do. He couldn't come up with anything, but then a couple of detectives visited him at his bakery and told him that they could and wanted to help for a small donation to the Policemen's Widows' Fund. "They actually asked for a pretty big donation," Uneeda confessed, "but I was desperate and I now had come into possession of Uncle Ebeneezer's legacy. I agreed and they said they would speak to their lieutenant, who in turn would speak to a certain assistant district attorney who was currently experiencing a minor cash flow problem. And it has all worked out. Mona will go free and some poor widows will benefit."

"Mr. Baker," I asked, "did these two detectives give you their names by any chance?"

"Well, not exactly. One of them, a Mediterranean-looking guy who was very fat and kept eating the pastry that was sitting out on the counter, did once call the other man 'Rip' or 'Ripper' or something like that. But they said they couldn't give me their names because J. Edgar Hoover wouldn't allow it."

O'Meara and Bruttafaccia. Why wasn't I surprised? I wished Mr. Baker all the best and then hung up on the jerk.

I sat around the office mulling over the injustices of the world and picking at a scab. Strangely enough, that gave me a thought: I had never asked Mona where the Llama and his gang were hanging out. Wherever it was, I'm pretty sure that they'd cleared out once their extortion scheme went bust and the cops picked Mona up. But maybe, just maybe, they'd left

a clue as to where they were now and where Dotty was
I grabbed my coat and hat, splurged for a cab, and head
the 17th Precinct where Mona was being held. On the
told myself that I'd have to pick at scabs more often.

25

I was getting nowhere with the desk sergeant, who said
that they didn't let just anyone walk in off the street and see
a perp who was in custody. I told him that I was a private
investigator. That got me less than nowhere, and he told me
to beat it or I'd be enjoying a nice comfy-cozy cell
compliments of the taxpayers. Then I told him to call my
good friend Phil Mazurki, who'd vouch for me.

"So why didn't youse say so in da foist place? Any pal of
a Polack is all right in my books." Then he called to another
uniform and told him to take me to the visitor's room and
haul Mona Tuvachevsky-Smith's skinny ass to see the
Polack's friend. I was amazed at Phil's clout. Maybe he
should run for mayor.

I didn't have to wait long before Mona arrived. I expected to see her dribbling a basketball, but it would have
been hard to do while wearing handcuffs. I guess the guards
got sick of her dribbling the ball, or maybe the perps in the
nearby cells complained. She had lost some weight and
looked uglier than ever, especially wearing her prisoner's
crab garb. I wondered not for the first time what Baker saw
in her. Oh well, they say beauty is in the eye of the beholder,
and he's the one who's got to hold her.

"You're looking good, Mona."

"Up yours, DeWitt."

She had a way with words. The good nuns at the Sisters of Pleurisy Convent School had taught her well.

"Listen, Mona, I know you're not nuts about me, but I need a favor."

She laughed so hard that my ears ached. A guard came in and asked if there was any trouble. I couldn't hear him at first but told him "no" once my ears cleared.

"Why should I help you, DeWitt? You got me here in the first place."

"No, Mona, the Black Llama got you here, and you know it. How did a semi-nice convent school gal like you ever get mixed up with a crumb like him?"

She put her head down on the table. I thought she was taking a nap but she soon looked up and glared at me.

"I might as well tell you," she said. "Why not? I'm getting out of the slammer in a couple of days anyway."

She proceeded to tell me that she had met him at a basketball game when her team, the Sisters of Pleurisy Shooters, was playing the Daughters of Sister Deirdre Dribblers. The Llama went up to her after the game and informed her that he was a scout from the Inca-Dinka Dunkers of the Pan-American Basketball Association and that he could get her "mucho dineros" for signing with him. She said he was real handsome, too, and that she was impressed that he spoke Spanish with a high-class Castilian lisp. Of course, she admitted, it turned out that he also spoke English with a lisp. He had heard about her from a former convent school classmate of hers, a girl named Gertrude who had a thing for gardenias.

"He told me that he gave this Gertrude some expensive gifts, but what she gave him in return he didn't care to mention in front of ladies. Anyway, DeWitt, that's the way it started, and you pretty much know how it ended. Some time after we'd met, the Llama came up with a scheme to fleece this mug I was dating, a dumb baker who doted on me, filled me with pastries, and promised me the moon. That should have been enough, but I got greedy. I wouldn't settle for the

123

moon and the pastries. I wanted the planets and all of the stars, and that's what the Llama said that we could have. Period. End of story."

Maybe I had got it wrong. Maybe Mona Tuvachevsky-Smith was just your normal, everyday, six-five basketball-dribbling dame who had gone wrong, had been suckered by a sweet-talking scumbag from south of the border. I was willing to give her the benefit of the doubt. At least for now.

I told her that she was really a good kid who traveled in bad company and that she could help me catch that bad company by telling me where the Llama and his pals were last residing.

She thought for a minute. "That'll cost you, gumshoe."

I wanted to reach across the table and smack her with the blackjack I was carrying. That lousy, good-for-nothing tramp. I had had enough. No more Mr. Nice Guy.

"Mona, the way I see it you have two choices. First, I can tell Mr. Baker, who's waiting for you like a pathetic puppy, that you've been screwing a couple of the guards here. Or—and I think I like this one better—I can arrange to have both of your kneecaps remodeled so that you can say so-long to your basketball dreams. Take your time and think it over. You got thirty seconds."

She spat in my face but gave me the address of the hotel where the Llama had been staying. I got up and left. I didn't bother saying good-bye, but then neither did she. I wouldn't expect a wedding invitation if Mona Sleaza and the baker tied the knot.

I waved farewell to the front desk officer, who told me to give Phil his regards and let him know if something good was coming up. I didn't ask what that might be.

The Hotel Buena Vista had seen better days, better months, and, as I viewed the broken stones and debris that littered its sidewalk and torn canopy, perhaps better years. It looked seedier than an Iowa cornfield at planting time. There wasn't much "buena" about the "vista" either. It fronted a firehouse and was flanked by an empty lot strewn with garbage on one side and a bowling alley on the other. From my analysis, my years as a tec led me to believe that few dignitaries stayed there. The Llama, of course, was not a dignitary, at least not in my book.

I pushed through a revolving door, which revolved with much difficulty. The small lobby complemented the hotel's exterior: shabby and depressing. The few chairs that failed to invite anyone other than moths looked like they had gone out of style with the sinking of the *Maine*. The hotel clerk looked as though he had been aboard that ship and had been one of the fatalities. He was nearly as pale as snow, one eye drooped sadly, and a scar marked the route from his right ear to his jaw.

"Hey, pal," I said, "I'm looking for some information."

He looked at me. "We got rooms here, not information. You want a room?"

I could have busted his chops, but it looked like someone had beaten me to it. I decided to play nice with him.

"Look, pal, if you fork over a little info then I can fork over some simoleons, if you catch my drift."

His eyes, or at least the one that didn't droop, brightened. "Say no more. What do you want to know?"

"I want to know if two Spanish-looking characters, one fairly tall and good-looking, the other average height with a real thin mustache, registered and are still frequenting this flea-bitten dump." I peeled off a couple of Washingtons.

"That's not much to go on," he said, looking contemptuously at the bills. "A lot of Spanish-looking gents frequent this dump, which, by the way, doesn't have fleas, only roaches. There are no pets allowed. This is a one-star hotel, for your information."

Yeah, and you're going to be seeing stars, I thought, if you don't give with the goods.

"Do you know that Washington's birthday is only a couple of months away? Here are some more pretty pictures of him," I said, tossing two more bills on the counter. He reached for them, but I whacked his fingers with my trusty blackjack before he could carry the moola to his pocket.

He cried out in pain and asked what I had to go and do that for.

I told him I was trying out for the U.S. Olympics blackjack team and needed to stay in shape. I added that this was my week for vigorous practice. He got the hint but not the latest installment of talk-for-pay.

I pocketed the Washingtons.

"There were these two greasers and a real tall broad who registered for a couple of rooms the week before last. The greasers were pretty quiet, but I had a helluva time with the broad. Other guests kept bitching that she was making too much noise bouncing a basketball, or some daffy thing like that. Since we don't have phones or elevators in this place, I had to take the stairs all the way up to the fifth floor night after night to tell her to cut out the noise. And me with my sciatica! I finally had it and was all set to boot her out, when I discovered that she was gone. Left all her things, too. I guess it was about the same time that those two guys also left, and without their things. They all must have slipped out at night because they never paid their bill. The bastards stiffed me."

I asked him if their belongings were still in their rooms. He said that the cops had come for them, although how they knew about the two men and the girl he couldn't fathom. Swell, I thought. Another dead end, and time was drawing shorter than my short hairs.

The clerk was tenderly rubbing his hand, which already was swelling and showing signs of discoloration. I felt a little bad that maybe I had overreacted. I reached in my pocket to give him those two bucks I had taken back. Then I thought of the five-thousand-dollar ransom the Llama was demanding. I couldn't see how I was going to raise that kind of money, but I knew there was no way in hell I could raise five thousand and two. I did give the clerk my card, however, and told him that if he ever needed a good gumshoe, just give a holler. He gave out a holler, but I don't think it was because he needed me.

26

Time was running out and so was my patience. The hotel lead had proved as disappointing as most of the broads I'd met since the ex and I had split. And that was pretty disappointing. It was a long way back to the office, but I decided to walk. Maybe that would stir some fresh thoughts. At the least it would save cab fare. I stopped for a quick lunch halfway back and had a liverwurst and mayo on rye, washed down by coffee so bad that even the patrons at Ma's would wince. That didn't bring any fresh thoughts either. My mood was so rotten that I told a Salvation Army Santa what he could do with his lousy bell. When some old busybody told me that I should be ashamed saying that to a Santa, and in public at that, I gave her worse.

The office was lonely without Dotty. I missed all that I had come to associate her with in the several years that she had been in my employ: poor typing, bits of odd clothing strewn about, fingernail and cuticle parings on her desk and the floor, lousy coffee, mindless questions and answers, books that she read but didn't understand. Maybe it wasn't much to miss, but I missed it, and I had to find a way to save her.

Making sure that the office door was locked, I went into the small room in the back and lay down on the couch, the one that from time to time I had unsuccessfully urged Dotty to enjoy with me. Without Dotty to cajole and too tired to think of anything save getting a catnap, I fell into a deep sleep. Then the phone rang in the other room and I fell off the couch. The damn thing kept ringing while I came to, figured out where I was, and managed to answer it.

"DeWitt here," I said in a sleepy voice.

"And it's Sadie Plotz here. How are you doing, handsome?"

"I've had better days, Sadie. What's up?"

"Besides you?" And she laughed. Sadie was always pretty good at double entenders or whatever the Frenchies call them. "Listen, sweetheart, you know the Spanish gal that works with me at the telephone office? Well, she says that two nights ago she spotted that Llama putz dancing up a storm at the Two for Tango Club over on the west side next to the meat packing district. What do you think? Should the two of us go tiptoeing through the tulips tonight and look for the lousy lowlife?"

Sadie didn't know about Dotty, and I didn't want her involved. This was something I had to handle myself, or maybe with Phil as backup. I told Sadie that I couldn't trip the light fantastic until I went to my chiropodist to have an ingrown toenail removed. I thanked her for the tip, however, and promised that I would look into it. She sounded disappointed but said she'd take a raincheck and give me private dance lessons at her apartment as soon as my ingrown toenail and I felt the urge.

I checked my watch. It was 4:10. I called Phil. No answer. I locked up, walked home, poured a Jack Daniel's, called Phil again. No answer. DeWitt, I told myself, you're on your own tonight. I had another shot of my friend Jack Daniel's—a short one this time—checked that my .38 was loaded for bear, and left. Once outside I felt a few snowflakes hit me. I went back upstairs and put on my galoshes. Who knew how much of the white stuff would be falling?

128

A Yellow Cab got me to Two for Tango. It was a nondescript place outside, save for a cardboard mannequin of a Valentino-looking character ogling his partner. I offered the hat check girl my coat, hat, and galoshes, and gave her a friendly shake when she extended her hand. The room was large, with a bar and a number of tables grouped around a medium-sized dance floor. Pretty good crowd for this time of evening, which said something for the place, although I don't know what. Some guy in a penguin suit asked me if I would like a table and held out his hand. This is a real friendly place, I thought, so I shook his hand, too, and headed for an unoccupied table across the way. He apparently thought I should wait for him to seat me, but I was tired and refused. When he insisted, I stepped hard on his foot, pulled at his bow tie, and told him that I'd turn his penguin suit into rags if he persisted. He got the message, and I got the table across the way.

I looked around. No sign of the Llama or Mr. Dough. A good-looking gal came up to me and asked if I'd like to buy her a drink. I said no. She wasn't that good looking. I kept trying to get the attention of various waiters so I could wet my whistle, but they seemed to be avoiding me. I wondered if Mr. Penguin Suit had anything to do with that.

The small band struck up "Hey, Rio." I was singing this catchy ditty, much to the annoyance of the couple seated next to me, when I spotted the Llama heading for the dance floor with some dame in hand. I jumped up, knocking over my table as well as the adjoining one in the process. The mug at the table shouted something not nice, so I took the time to cuff him a good one before I made a dash for the Llama.

The Llama must have heard the noise because he looked my way. His expression showed surprise. Then he flashed a mean smile full of glistening teeth, kissed his partner's hand, and rushed away. Not so fast, you punk from the Pampas, I thought. I've got you now. I kept pushing and shoving at the dancers as I pursued my quarry. He had a head start, but I was determined to catch him. By this time the place was pandemonium, and I could hear people screaming to call the cops. Mr. Penguin Suit tried to stop me and received a knee in the groin for his trouble. I gained some ground on the Llama and was finally able to reach for him. And then the lights went out.

They didn't come on again for a few hours, and when they did, I could see Sadie Plotz and a nurse standing over me. I wanted to go back to dreamland. My head throbbed and I couldn't blame the Jack Daniel's.

Sadie and the nurse were saying something to me that I couldn't understand. Finally the shifting pieces of the kaleidoscope more or less settled into place.

"Where am I?"

"Now just lie back and be still, Mr. DeWitt. You're here in St. Hieronymous the Healer Hospital. You have a nasty cut on your head and maybe a mild concussion, but Dr. Grosshandler says you're going to be fine."

Maybe, maybe not. I looked at Sadie, who was hovering over me, and asked what she was doing there.

"I was the one who called the ambulance and brought you here, Dick. Don't you remember?"

Of course I didn't remember. I asked her how and where she found me, and she said at the Two for Tango. Sadie looked rather sheepish—unusual for someone whose features always seemed lupine to me—and related how she had just arrived at the place when she spotted me pursuing the Llama. She grabbed an empty bottle that was sitting on a table, chased after us, and bashed the Llama over his head with her weapon. Trouble was that it was my head she bashed by mistake. "If only you had listened to me and we had gone together this never would have happened," she said.

Right, I thought. And if I hadn't been fooling around with you a few years ago this wouldn't have happened either. But I was too weak and too much the gentleman to rehash our history.

As my head increasingly cleared, my thoughts focused on saving Dotty from the clutches of the evil Black Llama. I said that I had to get out of the hospital and back to my place. The nurse and Sadie both tried to dissuade me, but I was insistent. I asked the nurse to call me a cab and refused Sadie's offer to accompany me home, where, she promised, she would make some chicken soup. I said I'd be happy to sample it on another occasion. She asked when and I told her soon. There went another lie.

The cab arrived in a quarter of an hour, and my two benefactors gingerly helped me inside. It was smaller and smellier than the usual ones, and when the cabbie asked "Where to?" I was tempted to say "Another cab." But I didn't. We reached my address, I paid him and went upstairs. Slowly, very slowly. It was 3:30 in the morning. What a day and what a night. At least it was over, and nothing more could go wrong. It was then that I noticed I was missing my coat, hat, and galoshes.

27

A gnat was buzzing near my ear. I tried shooing it away. I tried harder but without success. Then I realized that it was the phone ringing. It was Phil.

"Hey, Dickie, where the hell have you been? I tried calling you a couple of times late last night. Did you get lucky?" he chortled.

Yeah, I sure got lucky. I told him what had transpired and reminded him that the kidnappers would be calling. Not to worry, he said. He had the money and we would be prepared for them.

"You have the money?" I was incredulous. I might as well have heard that my ex-brother-in-law had picked up the tab at a restaurant. "Where did you get it?"

"Don't ask so many questions, buddy boy. I'll only say that it's not mine and it's not real. Okay?"

"Sure it's okay," I managed to stammer, "but what's all this about being prepared for them?"

The Polack let out a long sigh. "First you get the call from them telling you where the drop is. But make sure they let you speak with your secretary so you know she's still alive." I gave an involuntary shudder at the thought that she might not be, knowing that this was a distinct possibility.

Nobody in his right mind took a kidnapper at his word. "Once we know where the drop is, we move in."

"Who is the 'we,' Phil?"

Another long sigh. "You'll bring the money and I'll watch your back. I'll bring along a few friends, too."

This all sounded too easy and too good to be true, but it was the only hope, frayed though it was, to which I could cling. Phil asked where I'd be for the rest of the day if he needed to get in touch, and I said that I'd stay home rather than go to the office. Get some rest for tomorrow, he urged.

How do you get rest when you're restless, I wondered? Sure, my head ached like the Bambino had been using it as a fungo bat. But my mind was filled with the flotsam and jetsam of my life, where I had been, where I was at, where I was going, all of it ebbing and flowing and making me sort of queasy. I felt like tying one on, but I couldn't afford to cloud my mind any more than it was already. Bereft of booze, I somehow managed to get through the day, aimlessly if not painlessly.

I had set the alarm clock for earlier than usual but, as it happened, it wasn't necessary. I awoke just as the night was giving way to a wintry, leaden dawn. I threw on some duds and headed for the office while others were still reading their morning papers and tsk-tsking over the latest foul news. I reached the office even before Joe had arrived to man the elevator. It bugged me that the landlord still hadn't fixed the sign on my door, but I had bigger fish to fry today.

For the next few hours I didn't fry any fish. I fidgeted instead, waiting for the call that would send me into action. I fixed some coffee in the back room. It tasted better than the usual dishwater Dotty prepared, but I promised myself that I would put up with her bilge as long as I could get her back safely.

Ten o'clock and still no call. I sipped some more brew and stewed some more in my sour juices. Ten-fifteen. I was beginning to wonder if the Llama and Dough hadn't changed their plans. My blood ran cold as I imagined those Latin lowlifes selling my Dotty into white slavery and forcing her to spend her days as a prostitute. Why those dirty . . .

Rrrrnggg. It was the Llama.

"*Buenos dias*, Señor DeWitt. And how are you today, my friend?"

"I'm not your friend, Llama. Get that straight." Anger rose in me like oil gushing from a Standard Oil rig. "So let's get right down to business."

"So impatient you are," he clucked. "You *gringos* should take life easy. There is so much to enjoy, no?"

He was baiting me and enjoying every bit of it. I counted to ten in an effort to calm myself. Losing my temper wasn't going to help.

"Just tell me what I have to do to get her back," I said.

"Tonight you will bring me the five thousand dollars in what you people call unmarked bills. Don't have any bills larger than fifty dollars, *comprende*? You and the money will come alone. That is very important. If we see any signs that you have brought someone with you—*muerte*, the girl dies." He paused. "And that would be such a shame since she's such a lovely *señorita* with much beauty."

I could feel my anger surging.

"Where do we make the swap?"

"You know the old deserted pier that's next to Pete's Crab Shack? You meet me there at midnight. Until then . . . "

"Hey, wait a minute," I yelled. "I want to speak with the girl or the deal's off. *Comprende*? I wasn't born yesterday, you know."

"Oh, when was your birthday, *Señor*?"

"It was . . . " I realized that he was baiting me again. "Listen, Llama, you got the girl there or not?"

"But of course I do. I wasn't born—how you say?— yesterday either. Don't hang up the phone."

About fifteen seconds later I heard Dotty's voice. "Mr. D, Mr. D?"

"Yes, Dotty. Are you all right?"

"Yes, Mr. D," she sobbed. "I'm all right. But I sure wish I had my book to read."

She's kidnapped and the only thing daffy Dotty can think of is her book. "Just stay calm, Dotty, and everything will be just fine. You'll be free tonight."

"Do I have to be at work on time tomorrow, Mr. D?"

I asked myself why I was going to rescue her. Couldn't I let nature take its course? I quickly banished that ungenerous but reasonable thought.

"Don't worry, Dotty, you can have the rest of the week off."

"Gee, thanks, Mr. D. Will that be with or without pay?"

My rhetorical question now seemed more reasonable and less ugly. I decided to quit while Dotty was still ahead.

"Let me talk to the Llama, Dotty. I'll see you tonight."

The Llama came back on the line. I made sure that I had the instructions straight. Then I hung up. There were miles and miles to go before I could sleep.

I called Phil as I had promised to do once I had heard from the Llama. He kept muttering "good, good," as I recounted the Llama's instructions.

"Don't sweat it, pal. We'll have your Gal Friday back with you by the end of the evening and those two creeps wishing that they had never set foot north of the Rio Grande. Now here's what we're going to do . . . "

Phil said he would have a trusted friend bring the funny money in a suitcase and pick me up in front of my place at 11:00. Better to get to the rendezvous early since you never know what could delay travel even at that hour. Last evening he called our mutual friend Dilly Farkas, who agreed to do the driving.

"Unfortunately," said Phil, "Dilly called back early this morning and said he couldn't. His old lady broke his arm when she found out he got a little on the side. Dilly said she was mad as a wet hen. Under duress, and blows from the wife's rolling pin, he confessed that the episode had occurred when he drove you someplace or other last week. He told her a crazy woman had violently accosted him while he was innocently waiting for you in his cab. The wife promised him another broken arm and two broken legs if he ever had anything more to do with her or any other slut, and worse for you if she ever laid eyes on your ugly kisser."

Clearly, I had not read Dale Carnegie's *How to Win Friends and Influence People* carefully enough.

"But don't worry, Dickie boy, your driver will know what he's doing, and me and my guys will be cruising right behind you in another car. You won't be able to see us, nor will those crumbums we're going to nab, but . . . What's that?"

I could hear a woman's voice in the background. Phil said Louise wanted to say a few words to me and then I should go and relax and he would see me tonight.

"Hello, Dick? I just want to tell you to take good care of yourself, although I know you're big and strong enough to do so. I don't want anything to happen to you. You're such a nice man, you know that? We're going to celebrate when all this is over. So until then . . . "

It was a no-brainer: I'd take Louise over Mrs. Farkas anytime.

28

I had a dozen hours to kill—there I go using that word again—before the Polack's pal would pick me up. Stay calm, I told myself, the time would pass and I had to keep my wits about me. Dotty's life depended on that, and mine too. I checked and rechecked my .38 and took out some extra bullets for tonight. Couldn't tell if I'd be needing any or many.

Hanging around the office was getting me nowhere. Frankly, it was driving me nuts. I had to get out. I put on my coat, hat, and galoshes, which Two for Tango had returned to my office under my various threats of murder and mayhem. Then I beat the lunchtime crowd to a local chow house but wasn't in the mood for more than a BLT, some fries, and a cup of java. The time was dragging. I strolled a bit. The store windows, with their displays of holiday wares, interested me not a bit. Neither did the passersby heading to or from shopping or to or from filling their faces with food. I decided to take in a movie, any movie, just to pass the time. I bought my ticket and went in to see Jimmy Cagney in *Ceiling Zero*. Great little actor and dancer, Cagney. I had heard that this was a pretty good film, but you couldn't tell by me. My mind was too riveted on tonight's upcoming event to pay much attention to what Hollywood and Jimmy were telling me. I left the theater when the lights came on, unable to recall if I had chewed on a Mounds Bar or Almond Joy along with my popcorn.

It was almost dark when I exited. The December days were getting shorter and so was the time I had until I confronted the Llama. Yet I was in no hurry to get home. A drink or two and a chat with some of the imbibers at The Slippery Elbow beckoned, but I knew that I had to keep a clear head. There is a time and a place for hoisting my glass in tribute to John Barleycorn, but not now, not there.

It was only 5:00 when I got back to my apartment. Six hours left. Somehow they passed without my going out and buying some Old Golds, downing a few drinks at home, or opening the window and yelling, "I'm going to get you, Llama and Dough, you lousy bastards!" A bowl of Campbell's tomato soup and a few saltines I called supper. Then I showered for the second time that day. (Couldn't remember the last time I did that.) The radio played news, music, and a program or two, but don't ask for details. Ten forty-five. I couldn't take the waiting any longer. I made sure that my piece was in my coat pocket and my blackjack in my back trouser pocket, turned out the lights, locked the door, and went outside to wait for my ride and who knows what.

A dark Ford was parked directly in front of the building. The driver opened the window on the passenger's side and motioned for me to get in either the front or the back. I chose the latter.

"Howya doin'?" the driver asked. "Phil said I should come early 'cause you're a worrywart and would be outside the building early."

I told him that Phil had that one right. He told me that the funny money was in the suitcase next to him and that he would drop me off a few blocks from the pier so the bad guys wouldn't get suspicious. Phil and his party of heavy hitters would be right behind to make sure everything went the way we wanted it to. "You can depend on Phil," he said. As if I had a choice.

The driver—Stickshift Steve, he said to call him—eased the Ford in and out of traffic, neither speeding nor lagging behind so as to draw attention to us and our suitcase of fake ransom money. We got to our destination a half hour before I was due to arrive. He asked if I wanted to sit in the car for a while. I was too worked up. Besides, it might seem suspicious if I were being watched. The Llama had stipulated that I should come alone, and I didn't want to spit in the kasha, as some of my sheeny acquaintances so nicely put it. I thanked Stickshift Steve and got out of the car, along with the beat-up suitcase that Phil had provided.

A raw wind laden with drops of rain cut through me as I surveyed the rendezvous area. A fog was settling in, making it increasingly difficult to see what was what, let alone who was who. And it was dark. The city's lights shone in the distance, but the pier must have forgotten to pay its electric bill. My apartment had better lighting. But I figured that's the way the kidnappers wanted it: plenty dark. It was quiet, too, save for the cries of gulls and the sound of waves splashing. At one point I thought I heard the planks of the pier groan. Or was that someone crying out? Maybe yes, maybe no. I checked my watch. Eleven fifty-two. I started humming "I Cover the Waterfront" and then switched to "Slow Boat to China." Eleven fifty-seven.

"I see that you are punctuated, *amigo*. It is good to be punctuated."

It was the Llama. And he was punctuated, too. "Yeah, I got good manners. I'm always on time," I said. I couldn't see his face but was able to make out a human form, maybe ten or fifteen yards away.

"Then for your good manners you will be rewarded."

He began speaking in Spanish and a voice not too far away replied in kind. I couldn't see who possessed the voice but would have laid dollars to donuts that it was Dough's.

"Now, Señor Gummyshoe, we make what you call the 'swap'."

The Llama's flashlight picked up two nearby figures, Dotty and Dough. The former had her hands tied behind her. The latter was holding a knife to her pretty throat. Despite the evening's chill I was sweating like a pig. My right index finger, which had been on my gun's trigger ever since I heard the Llama's voice, was getting itchy.

"Let her go, Dough," I said, realizing then that I had a certain gift for poetic rhyme. "I've got the money here, so let her go."

"You think my *madre* she raised stupid *niños*?" asked the Llama. "We make the swap, the money for the *señorita*, at the same moment. That way everyone feel hunky-dory, or hunky-dunky, or howdy-doody, or however you say."

We agreed that the Llama would hold the flashlight so that Dotty, Dough, and I could come together. Once I showed the dough to Dough, Dotty would go free and we could all go our merry ways. Or so he said. Meanwhile, I was waiting for the Polack and his cohorts to come to our rescue and apprehend these two apes from the Andes. When would they make their move, I wondered. And how would they make sure that Dough didn't slit Dotty's throat? I wished I could whistle a Polish ditty and get Phil's attention, but I couldn't even whistle "Dixie" at this point.

"*Señor*," said the Llama, "I would like to go home and see my wife, my children, and my mistress for *Navidad*, if you please. So are we going to make the little swap or not? And, by the way, do not try anything or to be the hero. You are not Zorro, you know? While you and my friend are making the swap, I will have you—what you say?— 'covered'."

I realized that it was now or never, no procrastinating, no piddling. "I got you, Llama." I kept my right hand in my pocket on my .38, picked up the suitcase with my left hand, and walked slowly toward where the Llama's flashlight was pointing. I could hear footsteps. Then I saw Dough and Dotty. Dough still had his arm around her neck and a pretty good-sized blade at her throat. I put down the suitcase, opened it, and showed the funny money, which in the dark looked fully as honest as Honest Abe himself. Come on, Phil, I thought to myself, make your move. What are you waiting for?

"Now back away," the Llama instructed, "while my friend counts the money. It won't take long. He's used to counting money."

I did as he ordered, unsure as to my next move. Dough would probably be able to tell that the ransom money was fake. What then?

Just then a gull flew low and screeched as it passed overhead. Dough, who had been about to bend down and examine the ransom money, instinctively looked up. "Duck, Dotty," I yelled and hit Dough with a flying tackle I had used in a high school football game that had resulted in a broken collarbone for me when my intended target stepped aside.

"No, I think it was a gull, Mr. D."

Good old Dotty.

All hell was breaking loose. I was doing my best to turn Dough's face to pulp, the Llama was shooting wildly, and Dotty, I suppose, was looking for the gull. I sent Dough off to slumberland, took out my .38, and told the Llama that he'd better give up because he was surrounded by my friends, and I'd just as soon plug him with my .38 in any case. I didn't hear any more shots from the Llama, and I didn't hear the pitter-patter of oversized feet coming from the Polack and his crew. What I did hear was the sound of a motor boat starting up. I realized that this was to have been the means for the Llama and Dough to scram with the ransom money. Hampered by darkness, I moved hesitantly toward the dock, fired a shot in the air, and commanded the Llama to halt. The noise from the craft grew louder as it began to gather speed. "Until next time, when I will be sure to get you, *hombre*." And with those menacing words the Llama escaped. I knew that we would meet again.

I made my way back to check on Dough, who was still counting sheep or vicunas or llamas or whatever. I yelled to Dotty that the coast was clear.

"But I just heard a boat, Mr. D. The coast wasn't clear," she insisted.

I wanted to put some tape over her mouth but settled for untying her hands. She didn't seem the worse for wear, which was more than I could say for Mr. Dough. Even in the darkness I could make out that his face now looked more like the Frankenstein monster and less like Ricardo Cortez. I guess I didn't know my own strength.

"Hold it right there!" It was Phil, accompanied by three burly men, their flashlights shining on me. "Are you two okay?" he asked. "Where's the Llama?"

I explained all that happened and asked him why he had not arrived earlier. He gave a disgusted snort and said his car had hit one of the city's many potholes and had received a blowout. He and his men tried hailing a cab, but he knew that no sane cabbie was going to stop for four good-sized men who wanted to go to a deserted pier at night. So they had to make do with changing the tire.

Phil put some cuffs on Dough, who was just coming to, and tossed him into the trunk of his car as a prelude to dumping him off at one of the police stations. Then the six of us squeezed into the car. The two guys who were squeezing next to Dotty failed to complain. I kept asking for details of her ordeal. She kept asking about gulls—how many lived around the city, did they have many baby gulls, and could you keep one in your apartment. Go figure. I was glad we let her off first. I told her that the police would probably call her the next day but that she should take the remainder of the week off. I told her she needed the rest. I told myself that if I heard one more word about gulls I'd put an ad in the paper asking the Llama to come back and take her. Fifteen minutes later we arrived at Phil's former precinct, delivered Dough to the uniforms, and spent an hour or so telling our story and signing some papers. "You won't be leaving town, will you, because we'll have to talk with you some more," said one of the boys in blue.

"Nah, I won't be leaving," I said. "Only if I can help it." Then I walked out with Phil and the others. I said I'd take a cab home, but Phil insisted on driving me there. When I turned on the lights in my apartment, I realized that home never looked so good. The same went for my bed.

29

With Dough safely behind bars awaiting charges of kidnapping, and with the Black Llama on the lam for the time being, my life returned to routine, some of it good, some not so good, most of it pretty dull. Workwise, the only case that came my way was a two-day stint of tailing a businessman's wife to learn whether she was cheating on him. She was. There went another sap's happy holidays.

Meanwhile, Dotty, after taking a day off following her ordeal, returned to work, seemingly unchanged and untroubled. Oh yeah, there was one change. She appeared less obsessed with reading great works of literature. Her obsession had turned to gulls. Every day she brought in pictures of the feathered beasts for me to see and she talked about them incessantly. A case of gulls for the gullible, I noted silently. But at least I knew what I could give her as a Christmas gift: a secondhand book on gulls.

During these days after the rescue, I took advantage of slow time at the office (which, to be honest, was most of the year) to write a few holiday cards and do a little shopping. Joe the elevator man was going to get a bottle of cheap booze. That was easy. It was more difficult selecting a gift for Mom. But since she didn't like the can opener I had given her for Mother's Day, I was pretty sure that she would appreciate the new one I purchased at an upscale hardware store that had recently opened. After all, nothing's too good for good old Mom.

While my life was fairly humdrum now, big changes were affecting others. O'Meara and Bruttafaccia, I'm ever so pleased to say, were hauled up on charges of bribery and demoted. They're now walking beats somewhere in the worst section of the city. The Assburn was luckier. From what I understand, he faced even more serious charges but because of his connections in high places was allowed to retire on full pension. Any day I expect to receive an invitation to his retirement party.

And love is in the winter air here in our fair city. I got a call from Uneeda Baker, who said that he and Mona were going to get hitched. He wanted to tie the knot as soon as possible but said that she wanted to wait until the legacy from Uncle Ebeneezer was safely in the bank and earning interest. He said I could be sure that I'd receive an invitation to the wedding whenever it took place. I said that I wouldn't miss such a grand event for the world. And there goes another schlemiel, I told myself.

Love was also in the stagnant air of The Slippery Elbow. I went there one night and found Gardenia Gertie still with her arms around Hyman the Hebe. He looked happy as a you-know-what. I wished the two lovebirds well. They deserve to share a bit of the meager happiness that life doles out.

My pal Light Fingers Louie, on the other hand, was not enjoying the bliss of love or much of anything else, according to Gus, the watchful eye on the Elbow's guzzlers. Louie, he heard, had got involved in some scheme to disburden a safe of its contents and was now taking a vacation from town and his parole officer. Some cons kept clean noses. Louie's, I feared, would need a year's supply of Kleenex and still come up dripping.

Gus himself seemed in better spirits than usual, which wasn't saying much. The Elbow's dispenser of suds and assorted libations said that he was enjoying his stay on the sofa while his mother-in-law took his place in bed with his wife. This way, he said, he didn't have to hear the missus yelping and yakking when he was trying to get some sleep. The only trouble was now he had to look at two old bags instead of one in cold cream, curlers, and ratty bathrobes first thing in the morning. All but took his appetite for breakfast away, he complained. One look at Gus's paunch left considerable doubt that he had cut back on any meal. I also wondered how the missus and mother-in-law liked waking up to his grouchiness and less than Hollywood looks. But it was yuletide, and so I paid my tab and told him to have one on me. He said that he already had. That was the least a cheap shamus like me could do for him. And a Merry Christmas to you, too, I thought.

But I did wish my friend Sadie Plotz a genuinely happy holiday, in her case a Happy Hanukkah. I called to tell her about the Llama and Mr. Dough. She said that she was disappointed the former had escaped but pleased that I had nabbed the latter. She also said that we'd have to stop seeing one another, at least for a while. It seemed that she had just met a handsome rabbi, Gershom Gomorrah, and they had become an item. "Since when have you become religious?" I asked. She said that she wasn't religious but the rabbi was a mensch and he had "a great-looking tallith." I didn't pursue the matter.

But I did pursue matters with Polish Phil and Louise, who had helped me get through one of the toughest spots in my life. I invited them to a semi-swank restaurant to celebrate and to thank them for their help and moral support in the Black Llama caper, and also because I saw them as my friends. They say you can't have enough friends in life. Me? I've had too few. Anyway, I learned that night that Louise, much to my surprise, was not Phil's woman, but his cousin, who had left behind an abusive husband in Chicago and had come to our city to think things out. Phil had suggested to Louise that she invite the lowlife here and that they could subsequently sit on the terrace and watch the bastard's body float down the river. Louise would have none of that,

145

however. She decided that she would go back to the Windy City for one more try to patch up a marriage that never should have taken place. If it didn't work, she'd leave him for good. Maybe she'd return here, she said, since she adored her cousin Phil and, looking sweetly at me, very much liked one of his friends. I told her I hoped that she could salvage her marriage—I lied—but that part of me also hoped she would come back here to live. She reached across the table and pressed my hand. That was my early Christmas present, and about as nice a one as I could expect or deserve.

So here I am, a few days before Christmas, walking down the street toward my office and slightly on air, compliments of Louise. I still had to worry about the Llama and I had to make a big decision as to whether I should take a case that would send me to the West Coast for some time. Leave the only city that I have ever really known or wanted to know? And what if Louise came back and I wasn't here? I was in too good a mood to worry about anything at this point. Maybe the world wasn't such a bad place after all. I saw a Santa ringing his bell and wishing a Merry Christmas to one and all. I reached into my pocket and slipped him a buck. I thought of asking for some change back but didn't. I guess the Christmas spirit was with me. And maybe it was with my landlord as well. When I got to the office I saw that someone had been working on my door sign, which now read: "Dicks . . . Investigator." I figured that the person would complete the job. Or maybe he wouldn't.